'What do ... **required"?'**

A commandin... ...me into their conversation. 'I told you we were desperate for help when you rang.'

Jess raised her eyes to find herself confronted by an overwhelming masculine figure.

'I presume you are the person I spoke to?'

'Yes. I'm Nurse Fenn from the agency. Commonly known as Jess.' Her voice faltered as his dark eyes swept over her.

'Well, Jess—if I may call you that?' He clearly didn't expect an answer as he continued, 'As far as I'm concerned, you are indispensable. For today at least.'

Although a Lancastrian by birth, **Sheila Danton** has now settled in the West Country with her husband. Her nursing career, which took her to many parts of England, left her with "itchy feet" which she indulges by travelling both at home and abroad. She uses her trips to discover new settings for her books, and also to visit their three grown-up children, who have flown the nest in different directions.

Recent titles by the same author:

DOCTOR'S DILEMMA

A GROWING TRUST

BY
SHEILA DANTON

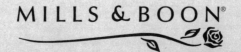

MILLS & BOON®

First published in Great Britain 1998
Harlequin Mills & Boon Limited,
Eton House, 18-24 Paradise Road, Richmond, Surrey TW9 1SR

© Sheila Danton 1998

ISBN 0 263 80798 3

Set in Times Roman 10 on 11 pt.
03-9806-55299-D

Printed and bound in Great Britain
by Mackays of Chatham PLC, Chatham

CHAPTER ONE

JESSICA FENN brought her 2CV to a standstill behind the blue Metro occupying one of the two spaces designated for Health Centre Staff.

The rows of cars filling every available parking space belied her belief that students barely existed on their grants. If the academic year was not yet in full swing, it was obvious that parking at Bradstoke College was going to be a nightmare.

Locking the driver's door behind her, she made her way confidently to the nearest entrance and studied the direction board until she found what she was looking for: 'Student Health Centre—Level One, Staircase A.'

Taking the route specified, she easily located the centre, and was about to push open the waiting room door when she heard raised voices.

'Is that the best we can do?' a querulous female voice demanded.

'I have more reason not to trust agency nurses than most, Lucy. I know it's not ideal, but what other option is there?'

Jess recognised the unmistakable deep brown tones of Dr Andrew Brent. But the warmth she had found so welcoming over the telephone only half an hour earlier was no longer apparent.

'Too right it's not ideal,' his female companion retorted. 'In my experience they want to work one day and not the next, and they refuse to do even one second above their hours. Even in an emergency.'

'I'm well aware of all that, but we can hope this one'll be an exception. The agency recommended her specially.'

'They would, wouldn't they? If we employ her, they get commission.'

'Have you another suggestion, then? You certainly can't cope alone, and it'll take time to find a permanent replacement. And at least she had a competent telephone manner.' Dr Brent's rising irritation at his decision being questioned caused Jess to visualise a middle-aged man who liked to get his own way.

Intending to confront them before the reputation of agency nurses was demolished any further, she pushed the waiting room door only to find it locked. She rapped loudly.

The door was opened by a nurse so petite that Jess felt a giant in comparison.

'Hi. You must be Lucy. I'm from the agency.'

Her friendly greeting was met by a pair of hostile green eyes set in a creamy complexion.

'I understood you needed a nurse when I spoke to Dr Brent earlier, but if you've changed your mind there's no problem. The agency have plenty of other work on offer.'

Jess watched the colour flare in Lucy's cheeks. 'No, er, you'd better come in and see Dr Brent.' Lucy nervously swept back a fringe of red hair that had fallen across her forehead.

Pleased to have wrong-footed the younger nurse, Jess murmured sweetly, 'If you're sure? But I do have a living to earn, so if I'm not required here, the sooner I get back to the agency—'

'What do you mean "not required"?' A commanding voice broke into their conversation. 'I told you we were desperate for help when you rang.'

She raised her eyes to find herself confronted by an overwhelmingly masculine figure. He filled the doorway of the consulting room on the left, giving Jess the distinct impression he was well over six foot.

Her earlier image couldn't have been more wrong. Although his hair, greying slightly at the temples, suggested he was approaching his forties, there was no way she could have described the lean and muscular frame, neatly clothed in a charcoal-grey suit, as middle-aged.

'I presume you *are* the person I spoke to?'

'Yes. I'm Nurse Fenn from the agency. Commonly known as Jess.' Her voice faltered as his dark eyes swept admiringly over her own imposing height, making her stomach flip.

'Well, Jess—if I may call you that?' He clearly didn't expect an answer, as he continued, 'As far as I'm concerned, you are indispensable. For today at least.'

The smile that accompanied his words didn't reach his eyes, and Jess shuddered inwardly as he made it clear he didn't expect her to be of much use.

Wondering what had happened in the past for him to distrust agency nurses so vehemently, Jess challenged, 'If I'm really needed, I'll stay, but it doesn't seem very busy at the moment, Dr Brent.'

She soon regretted her temerity as his cold gaze met her piercing blue eyes before raking slowly over her dark shoulder-length hair and the trim fit of her navy uniform dress.

His anger wasn't evident in his voice, however, as he cajoled, 'Students aren't early risers, Jess. The rush starts around ten. You'll see why we need you then. By the way, I'm Andrew and this is Lucy Robart.'

A stifled snort from his colleague distracted him. He shook his head ruefully. 'Lucy has had unfortunate experiences with agency nurses in the past.'

Irritated at his pretending that he had no doubts, Jess muttered savagely, 'I can assure you *both* we're not all the same.' And if I stay I'll make you both eat your words, she added under her breath.

He moved forward and grasped her hand. 'I'm sure *you* are very different.'

Annoyed at him using his sexuality to persuade her to stay, she snatched her hand away as if she had been stung.

'I guess you must have overheard our chat.' His voice

was now laden with entreaty, his lips curled into a smile of welcome. 'Please stay. And prove Lucy wrong.'

The nerve of him, Jess thought. 'There must be lots of nurses out there who haven't registered with an agency but who'd like to work regular hours with school holidays off. Considering your opinion of agency nurses, I would have thought one of those would suit you better.'

'Possibly. But how do we find them?'

'You could advertise.'

The dark-haired doctor nodded his agreement. 'It's already in hand. But it'll take time.'

'And that's something we don't have,' Lucy broke in, unconsciously smoothing the skirt of her turquoise uniform. 'Joanne took off at the worst time, with the new college year beginning and our receptionist-cum-secretary on long-term sick leave.'

'These things happen, as I guess you know.' His words were accompanied by a smile that still did nothing to convince Jess of his sincerity. 'Under the circumstances, I'm sure you won't let us down, will you?'

Lucy didn't give her a chance to reply. 'In that case, you'd better learn how our system operates before the rush begins.' She made the offer impatiently, clearly resentful that Jess had seized the initiative.

'Andrew's practice is similar to any other single-handed GP's, but as most of his patients are only here for three or four years his turn-over is much greater. That's what makes all the work.'

'How many students are studying at the college?' Resigned to staying at least one day, Jess dropped her bag and jacket onto the nearest chair.

'Over 4,000 full-time and many more part-time.' Lucy was eager to impress.

'How on earth do you cope with that number?' Jess was appalled.

Andrew reassured her. 'Thank goodness they don't all register with us. Some choose local GPs and some never bother. And, of course, the part-timers aren't our problem. They all remain with their own GPs.'

'And the staff?'

'We're a *student* health centre. Staff should all have GPs at home, even if they do often try to get a second opinion.'

'So the duties are similar to those of any treatment room nurse?'

'Dogsbodies, more like,' Lucy spat out with disgust, before locating a diary and proceeding to show Jess how to register patients and how to make appointments. She went on to explain curtly how to distinguish the few who were really ill from those looking for tender loving care.

'And there are plenty of candidates searching for TLC, I can assure you,' Andrew commented.

'I see.' Jess ignored his patronising tone as she tried hopelessly to understand the myriad of instructions.

Andrew must have noticed her struggle. 'I think we're swamping Jess with information, Lucy. Perhaps she'll find it easier to pick it up as she goes along.' Inclining his head towards her, he reassured her, 'A lot of it's common sense, but if you do find you're stuck either of us should be able to help you.'

'If we've a moment, we will. Otherwise you're on your own.'

Obviously worried that Lucy was about to undo all his attempts at persuasion, Andrew frowned his disapproval at her before asking Jess, 'Did you bring the employment papers from the agency?'

She nodded. 'I have them here.' She opened her bag, but he raised a hand to prevent her taking out the documents.

'I don't need them but the finance office does. If you turn right out of the waiting room door, it's the last office on the left. I should take them down now, before the rush begins.'

Jess set off slowly along the corridor, her thoughts a jumble of uncertainty. When the agency had mentioned Bradstoke College required a temporary nurse, she had leapt at the opportunity. The job offered regular hours, with no Saturday mornings, and it would be a bonus to work in a building of character after a four-week stint in the concrete edifice that housed an urban health centre. She had been required to work nothing but unsocial hours there, so was looking forward to being home regularly for Ruth's bedtime.

She had been even happier after speaking to Dr Brent on the telephone, and had felt that she could work with him. Now she wasn't so sure. However suitable the working conditions, she was not prepared to endure such hostility.

She handed her papers over to the finance officer with the terse ultimatum that she would possibly only remain one day.

As she was about to re-enter the department, however, she overheard raised voices for the second time that day.

Although she'd guessed Dr Brent had sent her to the finance office so that he and his nurse could discuss her position there, she was surprised to find she was again the subject of a heated exchange between them. She hesitated momentarily, her hand resting on the door.

'Remember, Jess's here to help us out of a spot, and not vice versa. After all, half a loaf is better than no bread. I'm sure she'd soon find another vacancy if she didn't stay here.'

His insult made Jess gasp, and then Lucy agreed maliciously, 'I'm sure she would, she only needs to flutter those baby blue eyes and any man will take her on. I'm not so gullible. Until I see proof of her ability, I'll reserve judgement.'

'That's fair enough. But as long as we don't expect too much of her, and keep an eye on what she's doing, how about we give her a try? Despite the colour of their eyes, there must be some good agency nurses around.'

'Huh.' If anything Lucy was even more disparaging. 'They only become agency nurses because they can't get a permanent job, or aren't willing to put themselves out when necessary. And on top of that they receive an inflated rate of pay. I'll bet she gets a much better hourly rate than I do.'

'It's the same with locum doctors.' Andrew Brent clearly shared Lucy's feelings.

'She's here to work,' Lucy told him defiantly, 'and I mean to see she does plenty. So don't be surprised if she can't stand the pace and doesn't return tomorrow.'

Jess determined there and then that, whatever the girl threw at her, she would stay and prove her competence to them both.

Smiling cheerfully, she entered the inner office. 'I've done that. However, I am worried about the confidentiality of your consultations. I heard every word you said as I came along the corridor.'

She was gratified to note Lucy flushing as Andrew hurried to reassure her. 'The consulting rooms are sound-proof—it's just this waiting area that has the grille above the door, so we never discuss patients in the office.'

'That's all right, then. Now, what would you like me to do first?'

A nervous gaggle of freshers entered Reception at that moment. Clearly embarrassed at having been overheard, Lucy thrust a batch of registration forms into Jess's hands and gave her a push towards the door. 'Register that lot to start with.'

Jess enjoyed the rapport she soon established with them. 'As new patients of Dr Brent, you all need to attend for a check-up. I don't suppose you know your timetables as yet, but when you do, bring back these medical questionnaires, completed, and we'll give you an appointment.'

Having dealt with the students to her own satisfaction, she was annoyed when Andrew began to pick holes in her work.

'You should have made them fill in the questionnaire before they left. That's one lot we'll probably never see again.'

'You have the details on their medical cards,' she retorted huffily. 'You can get in touch with them.'

Andrew shook his head. 'You'll learn, Jess. This is not like the cosy general practices you've probably worked at before. Students aren't so compliant. They are very elusive unless *they* want something. They never keep appointments and they move house repeatedly.'

Wondering how she was expected to have known that, Jess was stung by his criticism. So, as she had noted several patients arrive to consult Andrew or the treatment room nurse, she enquired, 'Would you like me to attend to those waiting to see a nurse?'

'A good idea if someone does, before the list grows any longer. I'll see my first patient now, Lucy.'

'About time, too,' Jess muttered under her breath as she entered the treatment area. After a quick check on the contents of the trolley and cupboards, she called the first name on the list.

The girl who responded looked so young that Jess was surprised to learn she was a second-year student.

'I'm Fran Gaunt. I've come for a check-up and a repeat prescription of the contraceptive pill.'

Confidently, Jess prepared to deal with the girl's request. This was something she was used to and knew she did well.

'How long have you been taking the pill?' Jess asked the question while wrapping a cuff round Fran's arm to check her blood pressure.

'Just over a year. My GP at home suggested it.'

Jess nodded. 'I expect he explained the reason we do this is to detect any early signs of side effects.' She rested the flat end of the stethoscope on Fran's elbow crease and listened for the beats measuring Fran's blood pressure.

Removing the earpieces, she smiled her reassurance. 'Absolutely normal; no problem there. Hop on the scales now. Fifty-seven kilos—is that about normal?'

Fran nodded, and then Jess went on to question the girl

about her general health. 'When was your last cervical smear test done?' she asked.

Fran's cheeks stained guiltily. 'I've never had one. I'm too scared.'

Jess smiled reassuringly. 'It doesn't hurt. A little unpleasant, perhaps, but when it can detect early signs of a cancer that can kill, surely it's worth it?'

'I do intend to arrange for one, but I've just started my bleed. Perhaps I could make an appointment, though.'

Jess nodded and went to check if smears were done at any special time.

Andrew's first patient had just left and Lucy was collecting the case notes from him. Mindful of being overheard, Jess joined them in the consulting room to voice her query.

'Surely you know they should be done halfway through the menstrual cycle?' Andrew queried with a suspicious frown.

'Of course I know that's when the most accurate results are obtained. I was merely enquiring whether you have special sessions, or if we just make an appointment when it's convenient to the patient.'

Lucy shrugged dismissively. 'If you want to make sure of doing it, I should get on with it now. We've already told you—students don't keep appointments.'

Jess raised a surprised eyebrow. 'Even though it's not the right time of the month? I think I'd rather take the chance that she'll show up in a couple of weeks' time.'

She lifted the appointment diary from the desk and swept back to her patient.

Having settled on a mutually acceptable date, she proceeded to see the next person waiting: a healthy-looking youth with his right leg in a plaster cast below the knee.

'Hel-lo!' He uttered the greeting breathlessly as his eyes swept the length of Jess's trim frame. 'You're new here, aren't you?'

Jess smiled. 'I'm just here temporarily. Now, what can I do for you today?'

'I broke my ankle on holiday, so I need to arrange to have this thing off.' He shook his right leg before continuing with a grin, 'But, for you, I'm sure I can think of something much more interesting.'

Used to dealing with that type of comment, Jess responded firmly. 'The leg'll be quite sufficient, thanks.'

Ignoring his rejoinder of, 'Pity', Jess went on to ask, 'Have you a letter for the hospital?'

At his nod, she continued, 'So you just want me to arrange an appointment?'

He nodded his agreement, but the flow of suggestive remarks continued. Jess ignored them and sorted out his hospital visit as quickly as she could. As he left, she was aware of Andrew watching from the doorway.

He joined her in the treatment room, closing the door behind him.

'Tim doesn't need any encouragement. He's capable of making a regular nuisance of himself without that.'

Outraged, she glared at him. 'Are you suggesting that I gave him some? I can assure you I've come across plenty of his type before. They just need firm handling, which is what I gave him.'

Andrew raised a suggestive eyebrow. 'You're obviously well experienced.'

Thrown off balance by his remark, she recovered herself sufficiently to ask briskly, 'Did you want something? If not, I have patients waiting.'

'Oh—er—yes. I've a chap in my surgery with torn ligaments in his right leg. I'd like you to strap it up. His name is Steve Jones.'

Jess's reply was excessively businesslike. 'Certainly. I'll help you get him across.'

Andrew went ahead, and Jess followed. She was surprised to discover a lad so tall that his head and lower limbs hung over both ends of Andrew's examination couch.

She turned to the doctor in mock horror. 'I guess my size must have been your main specification to the agency.'

Andrew laughed. 'It wasn't, I promise. But it certainly helps. How tall are you exactly?'

'Five-eleven. Now, up you come, Steve.' Jess turned to help the patient to a sitting position, then onto his good leg. 'Rest your arm on my shoulder and you can hop across to the treatment area.'

Andrew followed them into the treatment room, and as she set about the task she'd carried out so often he remained to watch. Used to working unsupervised, Jess found his presence unnerving, but, knowing it was a task she did well, she soon forgot he was there, and so was startled when he murmured, 'I can see you know what you're doing, so I'll leave you to it.'

His words encouraged her to believe she'd be left to carry out her consultations in peace for the remainder of the morning. She'd only seen one more patient, however, when he appeared again in the doorway.

'I've a girl in my room who needs her ears syringed, but we still use a metal syringe—not easy if you're used to more modern technology. Lucy can deal with this patient if you'd rather.'

Jess gave him a straight look. 'I *am* an experienced practice nurse, Dr Brent. Every health centre I work in has different equipment, but I can assure you I wouldn't attempt to carry out any procedure I'm not happy doing. As it is, I'm perfectly capable of using a metal syringe.'

Jess sensed Andrew was taken aback by her vehemence, but she felt it was justified after all she'd put up with.

It was nearly one o'clock by the time the backlog of patients had cleared, and she emerged from the treatment room exhausted, but satisfied she'd done a good morning's work.

'Are you going to the canteen for lunch?' Lucy queried.

'Well—er—I actually brought a sandwich.' Sensing it wasn't what Lucy had wanted to hear, she added hurriedly,

'But I don't mind where I eat it. I'll go down to the canteen or remain here and man the office if it helps.'

Lucy looked as if nothing Jess did would help, but didn't say so, although Jess soon gathered the reason for her antipathy. 'Andrew does that. He doesn't eat at lunchtime.'

Jess frowned. 'I'd have thought—'

Lucy interrupted rudely. 'When he finishes his day here he often has a game of squash or maybe goes for a run. He prefers to eat after that. You can stay here, if you like, but you'll probably be interrupted. I prefer to get away and meet people. It's all right for you, with someone at home, but I enjoy the company.'

Recognising Lucy was probing for details of her private life, Jess considered enlightening her, then decided it might be better to let her—and the doctor—believe she had a husband at home.

'Will you be using your car? I forgot to say I'd parked behind you. I presume the blue Metro is yours?'

An evil smile spread across Lucy's face. 'In that case you've probably been clamped. While I'm gone, you'd better ring Security and tell them it's yours. And when he's finished with that last patient, you can get Andrew his coffee. Men like to be waited on, as you no doubt know.'

Unhappy at Lucy's continuing enmity, Jess was thoughtful as she moved into the tiny ante-room to switch on the kettle. Even had a relationship *not* been the last thing she was looking for, Andrew was far too sure of himself to appeal to her. If that was what was worrying her, Lucy need have no fears on that front.

While she was waiting for the kettle to boil, the consulting room door opened and Andrew beckoned her. 'Kelvin needs a couple of sutures in a knee wound. He came off his bike on the way in this morning. It's right on the bend, so will heal better if it's stitched. Could you get things ready?'

'I can do the suturing if you like,' Jess offered.

Leaving Kelvin seated in his own room, Andrew followed her across to the treatment room. 'Have you trained to do this?'

She compressed her lips angrily before nodding. 'Do you *really* think I would offer to do it if I hadn't?' She sorted through the packs of sutures. 'You're welcome to watch,' she told him tartly. 'I *do* appreciate your need to be sure I'm competent in any extended roles I undertake on your behalf.'

'As long as you understand.' The long and searching look he gave her, before swinging round on his heels to bring Kelvin through from the other room, made Jess quietly confident she was starting to get her message across.

She grinned to herself as he helped the cyclist up onto her treatment couch. She scrubbed her hands and slipped on a pair of gloves.

As she infiltrated the area with local anaesthetic, she asked, 'What about your tetanus cover, Kelvin? I don't expect you chose a clean place to fall.'

Andrew answered for him. 'He makes a habit of falling off his bike onto dirty roads, so he knows the dangers of "lockjaw" better than most. He had a booster four weeks ago.'

She acknowledged the information with a nod, then drew the edges of the wound together with her first stitch.

When she had finished, Andrew snipped the thread for her.

'One more should do it, don't you think?'

He nodded. 'Fine. That should heal neatly.'

Her ministrations complete, Jess dropped the needles and syringe into a sharps box and cleared away the remainder of the debris.

'Don't forget to come back next Monday and have the sutures out,' Andrew called as Kelvin left.

'Well, did I pass muster?' Jess queried derisively while washing her hands.

He looked up from making the necessary notes on

Kelvin's case sheet. 'You sure did. I can see you're going to be more of an asset than we thought.'

'I could hardly be less,' she murmured drily as she reboiled the kettle.

He didn't respond, and, unsure if he was uncertain how to, or just hadn't heard, she took him a coffee. His fingers brushed hers as he took the mug from her hand and she was startled by a fluttering reaction deep within. She snatched her hand away, furious with herself for reacting that way to a man who didn't trust her or her work.

Glancing up, she found him watching her intently, so before he could read the effect he was having on her she returned to the ante-room, struggling to regain her composure before settling at the office desk with her coffee and sandwiches.

Despite telling herself that her response was nothing more than a physical reaction to his masculinity, she was still shaken by the forgotten sensual warmth permeating every fibre of her body.

Already aware that this job wasn't going to be easy, she guessed it wouldn't be helped any by her behaving like a love-struck juvenile—especially as she'd decided to give the impression that she was already married.

Most of the doctors and nurses she came into contact with through her work had known for a long time that she was a single parent with one child, and many knew Larry had died from the hepatitis he'd contracted as a medical student.

But the student health centre was clearly isolated from the local medical grapevine, so it was unlikely that Andrew and Lucy would know of her background.

'Now you've seen what we're like, are you prepared to stay with us until we fill the post?' Andrew called from his room.

Jess shrugged. 'It depends. I can't say I've felt particularly welcome so far.'

'It's nothing personal. I don't think Lucy will ever forgive Joanne for going off at this time. I'll feel quite sorry for her if she comes back.'

'Is that in doubt?' Jess asked, more for something to say than from particularly wanting to know.

'I'm afraid so. I don't expect to see her again. She's gone back to Scotland to help nurse her father. She's a family girl if ever I saw one and I think she'll stay up there. Not only to look after her father, but to help with the work on the farm.'

'Scotland? Bradstoke was a long way from home.'

'That's the main reason I don't expect her back. I've put an advert in the paper for a temporary replacement, but I expect it'll turn out to be permanent.'

'I hope you find somebody more acceptable than I obviously am.'

'Fishing for compliments?' Andrew emerged from his room and towered over her, his searching gaze this time allowing no escape.

Jess felt the colour flare in her cheeks as she rushed to deny the accusation. 'No-o, of course not. I—'

Lucy burst through the door at that moment, and couldn't miss the colour in Jess's cheeks, or the fact that Andrew was hovering between Jess's desk and the door to his surgery. 'Everything all right?' she asked suspiciously.

'Yes. Shouldn't it be?' Andrew returned abruptly to the seat behind his desk.

'You're back soon.' Jess tried again to be friendly, but the moment she uttered the words she knew she had said the wrong thing.

Lucy's eyes narrowed suspiciously. 'I don't make a habit of lingering over my lunch break.'

Jess felt pushed into defending herself. 'I didn't think you would, but canteen service can be diabolically slow. Would you like a coffee?'

'No, thanks. I'll make a pot of tea.'

Jess knew she was being snubbed, but, trying to ignore

it, asked, 'What would you like me to do this afternoon? There's no surgery, is there?'

'Not here, but on Mondays and Fridays Andrew and I visit our other site, and open up the surgery there between two and four.'

'So what is there for me to do here?'

'There'll be freshers to register, and there needs to be someone here to field any queries and deal with emergencies.'

'I see,' Jess said equably, although her expression spoke volumes. 'You'd better leave me with a contact number then; after only one morning something will surely crop up that I can't deal with.'

'Fair comment.' Andrew turned to Lucy. 'We can't expect Jess to cope alone until she understands our system. She'd better come to Roundings with me and you can hold the fort here for once.'

Lucy's expression was black as she emerged with her mug of tea. Allowing Jess any more time alone with Andrew was obviously the last thing she'd intended. And, if she was absolutely honest with herself, Jess wasn't too keen on it either.

CHAPTER TWO

ANDREW reversed a white Granada from his named parking spot and drove carefully over the speed retarders scattered along the college road.

'I can't understand why all these new college buildings have to be so ugly. They don't fit in at all, and if they continue to build them the beautiful proportions of the old building will be lost in the resulting concrete jungle.'

'I certainly prefer the main building,' Jess agreed.

'I wouldn't be surprised if they don't knock it down one day and replace it with another indistinguishable sky-scraper.'

Surprised by his outburst, Jess studied his profile closely, but although its clean-cut lines caused her heart to miss a beat, she read nothing enlightening there.

She waited until he'd turned out of the gate before asking, 'Why does the college have two separate sites?'

He shrugged. 'They were two individual colleges that amalgamated. There was no room to move the newly acquired faculty onto the main campus—a situation that will no doubt be resolved in the near future. The split site is not ideal.'

'Do all the students at Roundings study the same courses?'

'More or less. Surveying and its allied subjects. I keep hoping that the big chiefs there will stick out for a building with character when they move. But it's probably too late. It will no doubt conform to the modern pattern.'

'How far apart are the sites?'

'Only a couple of miles, but through town traffic—which means it can take up to half an hour on bad days.' Needing to concentrate on his driving, he didn't say anything more, so, opening the warm jacket she had donned against the autumn chill, Jess relaxed into the seat, enjoying the luxury.

'Like it? The car, I mean?'

'It's great. I'm not used to a car being comfortable.'

He frowned. 'Why, what do you drive?'

Jess shrugged nonchalantly, hoping to convince him that it wasn't important. 'Didn't you see it? I parked it behind Lucy's.'

'The 2CV?' He was plainly amused.

'I'm afraid so.'

'Why be afraid if it gets you from A to B? But didn't you notice it was wheel-clamped?'

She clapped a hand to her mouth. She'd been so busy concentrating on the afternoon ahead that she hadn't looked. 'I forgot—Lucy told me to ring Security while she was at lunch, and then Kelvin needed those stitches and it went right out of my mind.'

'I thought it belonged to a student and that it served them right.'

'I don't want to be delayed this evening. I must contact Security the moment we get back.'

'No problem. We can ring from here.'

He swung in between a pair of heavy stone gateposts to park in front of a building that was even older than the original part of the main site.

Jess gasped with delight. 'I'd no idea this was here. Just look at those rosebeds. And that doorway. It's beautiful.'

'And unspoilt by development. How long that'll be allowed to continue, I dread to think.' Handing her a bewildering bunch of keys, he swung his briefcase from the back seat of the car and, after securing the doors, led the way in through the main entrance.

Jess looked up at the high ceiling. 'What fantastic mouldings.' If this was what the corridor was like, she couldn't wait to see the rest of the building.

Andrew was obviously pleased by her appreciation. 'Yes,

and I'm prepared to lay odds that this'll be the first time you've worked in a surgery with a stained glass window.'

'Stained glass?' echoed Jess. 'I don't believe it.'

'Well, I suppose I am exaggerating slightly,' Andrew laughed. 'The glass in the surgery door is coloured and arranged in a pattern that prevents peeping Toms.' He studied her intently for a moment. 'Are you interested in old buildings?'

'When I get the chance. They have a warmth that modern designs seem to lack.'

He rested an appreciative hand on her shoulder. 'Good to have you along. Most people moan about the inconvenience.'

Wondering if Lucy was one of them, Jess felt a pleasurable warmth that they at least shared one common interest.

They came to a halt in front of double doors which Jess instantly knew must lead to the surgery. The upper half of the heavy oak doors fitted Andrew's description perfectly. She tried to peer through one of the small diamond panes, but found the images were distorted.

'You need the large key at the left of the bunch to unlock the door.'

Jess found the one he meant and let them both in.

She was surprised to discover relatively modern consulting room fittings.

Laying his briefcase on the desk, Andrew held his hand out for the bunch of keys. 'I'll unlock your desk and show you what's where, then we can explore the hidden delights of my room.'

Jess placed the keys on his outstretched hand, expecting him to show her which key to use. Instead, he dropped the bunch onto the desk and, grasping her wrist, pulled her towards him.

His touch caused a similar sensation to flood Jess's body as had startled her earlier in the day. She panicked momentarily, but he merely turned her around and gently pulled back her head. 'Drink your fill of that circular window above the door.'

Jess gasped, thankful to have something concrete on which to pour out her feelings. 'It's beautiful, Andrew. What does it depict?'

She turned to look at him, but, discovering his attention focused on the circular window, she returned her gaze upwards.

'Jesus washing the feet of his disciples. I don't know if you are aware that until recently this was a church-affiliated college?'

'I didn't know that, although it was very often the case, wasn't it?'

'It was. I must say it's a refreshing change to find someone so knowledgeable in a place like this, where they believe anything old equates with bad. One day, when we have time, I'll show you a proper stained glass window upstairs.'

His words suggested that he expected there to be another opportunity, and they were endorsed by a subtle hardening of his muscles where they were in contact with her back.

Her thoughts scudding wildly, Jess moved away from close proximity as soon as she could. There was no way she was prepared to lose control of her emotions after managing to keep them on a tight rein for almost seven years. Apart, that was, from those she lavished on Ruth.

When she had learnt of Larry's death, her postnatal misery had caused her to blame herself, and so she had made a solemn promise to his memory that she would devote herself solely to their love-child. Or at least until Ruth was old enough to take charge of her own life.

Doing so had helped Jess to come to terms with her loss, and, though she now accepted his death without the initial crushing burden of guilt, she wouldn't allow herself to even entertain the thought of another relationship.

Andrew must have sensed her internal conflict. He regarded her steadily for a long moment, then, as if mentally jolting himself from a reverie, demonstrated which keys fitted the various drawers and cupboards before unlocking the door into his surgery.

'We've wasted enough time. You'd better get down to work. It must be nearly two.' His brusquely spoken words were in sharp contrast to their rapport of a few moments earlier.

'What would you like me to do?' she asked archly.

'Book the patients in and register the new ones?'

'That's probably all you'll be able to cope with initially. It needs to be done carefully and accurately if we're to keep track of all our patients.'

Incensed that he still felt the need to treat her as potentially incompetent, Jess glared at him in silence.

'There's no waiting room here, and no treatment room, so there's not much else you can do—unless I call you in to assist me. Which I'll certainly do if I need strapping or bandages applied. *They* are not my strong point.'

A knock on the outside door prevented further conversation and the surgery opened with a group of girls arriving to register.

'I'll just go and ring Security about your car,' he murmured as she invited them in.

Jess was surprised, but grateful, when he joined her and helped with the paperwork, but she didn't allow him to see it.

The moment one of the girls asked for a consultation with the doctor, however, he returned to his surgery, taking his patient with him.

Jess was pleased to discover how easily she coped, without bombarding him with endless queries.

Halfway through the afternoon he called her in to act as chaperon while he examined a second-year student. 'Maria has von Recklinghausen's disease,' he told her. 'I like to check her over regularly.'

Jess racked her brain to recall what he was talking about, and wondered if he had mentioned it deliberately, so that she would have to show her ignorance and ask. While the young girl undressed, however, Andrew reminded her.

'Apart from the brown patches on her skin, and the odd lump and bump, Maria was symptomless until her first year here, when she had difficulty walking.'

Of course. Skin pigmentation and multiple benign tumours of the nerves under the skin surface.

'She had a neurofibroma removed from her spine last year and she's now doing very well.'

Maria grinned. 'Dr Brent guessed what the problem was on my first visit. My doctor at home thought it was all in the mind. Wanted me to take anti-depressant tablets because he thought I was homesick.'

Andrew was checking Maria's skin for sensation. 'I probably have more time per patient than most GPs, and so I carried out a full check of her nervous system on her first visit. Something her doctor at home would have done if the tablets hadn't done the trick.'

Maria grinned up at Jess. 'He tries to hide his light under a bushel, but I think he's wonderful. Don't you?'

Jess was relieved to be able to say, 'This is my first day at the college.'

'You're in for a treat, then.'

'That's quite enough hero-worship for one day, young lady. You're fine.' As Andrew moved across to his desk, Jess noticed he was slightly disconcerted by the excess adulation. Something she wouldn't have expected from her first impression of him, and for some unfathomable reason she was pleased by it.

The remainder of the afternoon passed in a flurry of paperwork. When she ushered in his last patient it was well after four, so, to prevent further interruption while she cleared up, she snapped the lock on the outer door.

'Could you come in a moment, Jess?'

She joined Andrew in the surgery to discover his young patient reclining uneasily on the consultation couch, his complexion pallid.

'I need a blood sample from Ian, but even the thought caused him to keel over. Could you hold his arm still and distract his attention for a moment?'

Jess did her best, asking the boy what he was studying and whether he played any sports.

'I used to be in the rugby team, but at the moment I've so little energy I can't even complete a training session. Goodness knows what's wrong with me.' Ian was obviously worried and Jess tried to reassure him.

'You've probably been overdoing it. What year are you?'

'Final.'

'So, have you spent the summer working at your books?' Andrew asked.

'In what little spare time I had, yes. But I had to work for my living during the day. I was so overdrawn I couldn't have continued my studies if I hadn't.'

'What did you do?'

Ian grinned for the first time. 'I served baked potatoes from a seafront stall, working all the hours God sent.'

'No wonder you're exhausted.' Andrew shook his head. 'I'm amazed you were able to study at all after hours like that. He leaned over to pat Ian on the shoulder, his movement emitting a subtle waft of a heady aftershave into the atmosphere. 'All finished now.'

Struggling to ignore her renewed awareness of the doctor, Jess started to help the youth to sit up very slowly.

'Don't rush him, Jess,' Andrew ordered sharply. 'There's no hurry.'

Aware that rushing Ian was the last thing she would have done, Jess sighed deeply. When she was satisfied all was well, she helped him to transfer to the chair at Andrew's desk.

'Right, my lad, there's nothing more we can do until we get these results in a couple of days, so in the meantime I suggest you go back to your room and rest. No sport and no exertion.' Andrew checked Ian's address on his records. 'Still at Highstream Road?'

Ian nodded.

'We could drop you off there on our way back to the main site. And we'll call with your results on Wednesday if they're through. That should save you exerting yourself more than necessary.'

Ian appeared relieved, but then mentioned tentatively, 'What about lectures? I've a full day tomorrow.'

Andrew reassured him. 'I'll speak to your tutor. Give the lectures a miss until we get the results of these blood tests. Then we'll take it from there.'

As Jess had already tidied the outer office, they were able to leave almost immediately.

She chattered to Ian until he was dropped at his front door. As Andrew drove away from the terrace of dilapidated properties rented out to students, she asked, 'What do you think is wrong with Ian?'

Andrew didn't answer immediately.

'I don't want to commit myself, but it could be a kidney problem. I think he may have left it longer than he should to consult me.'

'You mean he's heading for kidney failure?'

'Maybe, but it's only speculation. I don't know if you noticed the lemon tinge of his skin?'

'No, just that he was very pale.'

Andrew nodded. 'His blood pressure is raised and he's unnaturally lethargic, as well as complaining of nausea and skin irritation.'

'Poor Ian.'

'I certainly didn't give him any idea of my suspicions. If it's not kidneys, it could be a pretty severe blood disorder.'

'In his final year too.'

'Pretty traumatic at any time. Not a typical day in the life of a college doctor. I often do a whole morning's surgery without discovering a genuine case of ill health.'

Jess smiled her acknowledgement. 'That's not confined to college students. I've known many GPs say the same.'

Andrew nodded. 'The occasional patient like Ian makes it all worthwhile. If we can help him back to health, we'll have earned our keep.'

Jess began to wonder if her first impression of him had been a little harsh. His appreciation of fine architecture, together with his high standard of care for his patients, made her appreciate his intolerance of nurses with no interest in their work. But why he should believe they all worked for agencies, she couldn't imagine.

When they arrived back at the main Cobbold Road site, she was delighted to see that her car was no longer clamped. 'Thank you for arranging for my car to be set free.'

'No problem.' Andrew checked his watch before helping her from the Granada. 'As you finish at five, there's little point in you coming back into the surgery now, is there?'

His question suggested to Jess that he expected her to be a clock-watcher, so she offered, 'If there's something more to be done, I don't mind staying on.'

'I thought you said you didn't want to be delayed this evening?' His dark eyes smouldered with an emotion that Jess was unable to interpret.

'I'll work as long as necessary.'

He frowned. 'There's no need. The students all disappeared long ago. See you tomorrow?' Although he phrased the statement as a question, he obviously expected an affirmative answer.

'You start at nine?' Jess answered him with a question of her own.

'Yes.' He paused before asking, 'Do you have ties that'll make such an early start difficult?'

Jess retorted irritably, 'I can be here on time. There's no problem.'

'So why do you do agency work?' His eyes narrowed as he probed for the answer she'd just evaded giving.

Finding her response difficult, Jess's reply was hesitant. 'I'm a single parent.' Aware of the look of disapproval flashing across his face, she rushed on to explain, before he could think she had a latch-key child at home. 'Don't get me wrong. I do have help with my daughter, but I like to be available should there be a problem. She's my responsibility, so it wouldn't be fair on an employer to work full-time.'

A puzzled look crossed Andrew's features. 'Who's looking after her at the moment?'

'Her grandmother. We live with her.'

'That's your mother?'

Jess felt the questioning had gone far enough, so she shook her head and, before he could ask anything more, said, 'I'll see you at nine tomorrow, then.'

'Well, if you're sure. But take your time. Come in when you're ready.'

His understanding suggested to Jess that he was used to dealing with a family of his own, but, not wanting to prolong the conversation by asking, she said, 'Nine will suit me fine.'

As she made her way out of the car park she was surprised to see he hadn't moved, but was watching her with a look that, if she hadn't just clambered from the luxury of his Granada, she would have believed expressed envy.

Telling herself not to be ridiculous, she parked the car in front of the stone-built Victorian semi that was now her home, and pushed all thoughts of him from her mind. Ruth was the most important person in her life, and this was *her* time.

She smiled indulgently as she lifted a hand in acknowledgement of her daughter's eager wave, and, ignoring the fact that the child was perched on the windowsill, a habit usually discouraged, she rushed inside and gathered the little girl into her arms. For some reason one day at the college had unsettled her in a way she wouldn't have believed possible. A homely evening with Ruth was what she needed now, to get things back into perspective.

'Difficult day?' Gwen Halton entered the room, unnoticed by either mother or child.

'Different, at least. I'm working in the college surgery. It's a general practice really, but that's where the similarity ends. There are no evening or weekend surgeries, but the turn-over of patients is colossal with the start of each academic year.'

Gwen nodded her interest. 'Will you be there for long?'

'As long as it takes for them to fill the post, I guess.'

'It sounds ideal for someone in your position. *You* ought to apply for it.'

Without answering, Jess sat down to listen to Ruth telling her all about her day's activities.

'I made this at school.' The little girl produced a battered egg box which purported to be a jewellery box.

'That's lovely, dear.' Jess handled the box as if it held the crown jewels. 'You are clever. Have you had your tea?'

Ruth nodded. 'And we put the kettle on to make some for you. Didn't we, Granny?'

Gwen smiled her agreement and went to fetch a cup of the reviving brew for Jess.

She took a sip and smiled her gratitude. 'You don't know how much I needed that. When I've finished drinking it, we'll get you bathed, my girl, and into bed.'

When Jess had read Ruth three stories, and all was quiet at last, she joined Gwen and her husband, who were waiting patiently for their evening meal.

After Gwen had served them all with the main course, she told her husband where Jess had been working all day, before repeating the suggestion Jess had evaded earlier. 'Why don't you apply for the job permanently? It would mean you'd be home every evening for bedtime.'

Jess grimaced. 'It's not as easy as that. The position they're advertising is only temporary, and I can't afford to be without an income. And anyway, I don't think the girl I would have to work with would want me.'

Gwen was scandalised. 'Why ever not?'

'I suppose you could say we didn't hit it off.'

'What about the doctor?'

Jess sighed deeply, 'He doesn't think much of agency nurses either, and it's probably just as well. If he did, the full-time nurse would probably like me even less!'

'Huh. I should take no notice of that if it's a job that gives you weekends and the school holidays off and—'

Les Halton's attempt to join the conversation for the first time was cut short by his wife. 'You mean he isn't married?'

Jess shrugged. 'I don't know. I presume not.'

'So I can't see any problem—especially as being a practice nurse you work mostly on your own.'

'Some of the time, but—'

'But nothing,' Les Halton broke in gruffly, determined this time to have his say. 'I think Gwen's right. You've had enough of this agency lark. We'd both like to see you settled in a regular job with reasonable hours. You deserve a break.'

Jess flashed him a smile of gratitude for his support. 'That still doesn't answer the problem of time off when Ruth's ill.' She shrugged helplessly.

'That's no problem now she's older. I can easily look after her.' Gwen would brook no argument.

Jess smiled. 'You're gluttons for punishment.'

'We're just grateful you give us the chance to spend so much time with the only grandchild we'll ever have. It eases our loss.'

Jess leapt to her feet and flung her arms around Gwen in a warm hug. 'I'm the lucky one. Goodness knows what I'd have done if you two hadn't offered me a home with built-in babysitters.'

Gwen kissed her fondly. 'After Larry died we had nothing to live for. You and Ruth have made life bearable again.'

Jess settled back in her chair. 'All the same, I can't expect you to do everything.'

'Now she's at school we do very little. You just see how you get on in the next few days, and if you think you'd like that job, we'll be here for Ruth. Never fear.'

After the meal was cleared away, Jess made her way up to her own room in a thoughtful mood. When Larry had died, she'd thought it was the end of her world. She remembered only too clearly how the maternity ward staff had tried to find out his whereabouts, but in the end had admitted defeat.

If only they'd known he was in a hospital not a hundred miles away. He had contracted a dose of hepatitis that had killed him within days of developing the symptoms.

It was her perennial regret that he hadn't known of Ruth's birth, but she could make up for it by allowing his mother and father as much access to the little girl as they wanted. And it helped her too. It meant she could get out and earn enough money to support her daughter without the usual worries of a single parent.

She was too wound up to sleep well, but nevertheless was up early enough to take Ruth to school before reporting for duty at the surgery at nine. At least arriving early ensured she had a parking space!

When she opened the waiting room door, Lucy looked at her in surprise. 'I didn't expect you yet.'

Jess lifted a shoulder non-committally. 'Why ever not? You start at nine, don't you?'

'Yes, but I thought you'd have to see your daughter settled wherever you leave her before you came.'

'I've done that,' Jess informed her quietly, aware that Andrew had lost no time in informing Lucy of the reason for her doing agency work.

Lucy was taken aback. 'Oh. I see. Well, now you're here there are a couple of girls waiting to see a nurse.'

Jess grinned to herself as she entered the treatment room. One Brownie point for the agency nurse account!

She called in the first student, who was miserable and complaining of a sore throat. After only a short chat to the girl, and an examination that revealed nothing of note, she recognised the girl was homesick. Needing TLC, as Lucy would put it!

Sitting her down, Jess asked, 'What are you studying, Andrea?'

'I only arrived two days ago. For the Social Science course.'

Jess could see the tears trembling on the brink of her eyelids, and hastened to reassure her patient that many students felt this way in the early days.

When she eventually felt she was gaining the girl's confidence, she began to describe the variety of social activities provided within the college. 'Have you met any of the others on your course yet?'

'No. The students in my digs all seem to be on the science side.'

'I shouldn't worry about that. As you settle in, you'll realise it's best not to live with people on the same course or you never get away from it. When are you due to register?'

'This morning. But I don't think I want to now.' This time the tears spilled over and trickled down her cheek.

Jess handed her a tissue from the box conveniently sited on the desk. 'Of course you do. That'll be your chance to meet some of those who'll be studying with you. And you'll probably find many of them feel exactly as you do.'

'Do you really think so?' Andrea raised wet eyes hopefully.

'I'm sure of it. It'll make all the difference, and you can all go together to the Freshers' Fair this afternoon.'

At Jess's confident prediction Andrea's face brightened. After a prolonged and thoughtful silence, she dried her eyes and made a move towards the exit. 'Perhaps I'll go and register, then.'

As the door closed behind her, Jess murmured quietly, 'Let's hope they're all as easy to deal with.'

'But that they don't take so blinking long.'

Jess whirled around to discover Lucy had joined her in the treatment room. 'Do you realise there are so many waiting for your ministrations there is not a free seat out there? You'd better get a move on or we'll have a riot.'

Jess felt the colour flood to her cheeks at the criticism. She knew she couldn't have helped the girl in any less time, so there was no way she was prepared to defend her handling of the case. Instead, she ignored Lucy and called in the next student.

The next three patients had simple problems to resolve, and Jess dealt with them quickly, only to find the fourth was another student needing time and TLC. A male this time, who Jess found difficult to believe was much above sixteen.

She sat him down and listened to his problems for a full twenty minutes before she could even get a word in. She had just started to talk to him, as she had to Andrea, when she was conscious of the door from the office opening again.

Determined not to allow Lucy to rush her, if anything she took longer with Keith, cajoling him and reassuring him that by the end of the week things would look very different.

When he eventually went off, much happier, she turned for the confrontation with Lucy to discover Andrew leaning against the wall, watching her speculatively.

Feeling the colour rush to her face, Jess stammered, 'Oh, I'm sorry, Andrew. I didn't know you were waiting. I thought Lucy had looked in. What was it you wanted?'

'Nothing that couldn't wait. What you were doing was much more important. It obviously helps to have a child of your own.'

Jess laughed dismissively. 'I can assure you I haven't reached this stage with Ruth as yet.'

'Ruth. That's a nice name. Did you choose it?'

Jess nodded, wondering how on earth the conversation

had swung round to her daughter when there was still a queue of students waiting to be seen.

'If there's nothing I can do for you, I'd better get on. Lucy will be—'

'Wondering where I've got to,' Andrew finished for her, as the door opened to reveal the subject of their conversation. 'Finished that dressing, Lucy?'

Obviously far from pleased to find them chatting while she worked, she snapped, 'I've just seen him out. If I'd realised Jess was free, he could have come over to her instead of delaying your surgery.'

'No problem. It gave me an opportunity to see what Jess was up to.' He ambled across to his room.

Irritated that, despite knowing why she did agency work, he still felt the need to monitor her work, Jess called in the next student waiting to consult her.

She was thankful it was nothing more than a routine check-up for a girl on the contraceptive pill, because Lucy slammed the door as she left, leaving Jess to wonder why she'd bothered to return for a second day in such a hostile atmosphere. There was plenty of work available with the agency at the moment, so she didn't *have* to stay.

Having dealt with the check-up quickly, Jess called in the next patient. Russell was a new student, who had only arrived in the area two days before and had been feeling ill since eating a curry on Sunday evening.

She questioned him closely, and the history he gave of stomachache and vomiting pointed to a simple connection between his illness and the curry. And yet there was something about his condition that hinted to Jess that it might just be more serious.

'Hop up onto the couch and let's have a look at your tum.' He did as he was asked and slid his jeans down a fraction, obviously embarrassed. 'Have you still got the stomachache?' Jess asked him quietly, having noticed the discomfort mirrored in his face as he moved.

He nodded. 'It's not as bad as it was, though.'

'Whereabouts do you feel it?'

He ran his hand vaguely across his upper abdomen. 'Around here to start with, but now it seems to be lower down.' He pointed to the right side of his abdomen.

Warning bells rang immediately in Jess's mind, and she wanted a second opinion. Andrew would need to examine him, and there was no point in her embarrassing the lad further by doing so herself. She covered Russell with a blanket and told him to lie quietly for a few minutes while she had a word with the doctor.

She closed the treatment room door behind her and asked Lucy if Andrew was free.

'Not at the moment.'

'I'd like him to take a look at the lad I've got in the treatment room—Russell Derwent. He's a fresher.'

'Send him into the waiting room, then, and he can go in next.'

Jess shook her head, conscious that she couldn't say much without being overheard. 'I'd rather not,' she whispered. 'He's not all that well, and as he's already lying down I don't want to disturb him too much.'

'But he's blocking the treatment room,' Lucy hissed impatiently.

'I'm know. I'm sorry.'

'A fresher, you say? Are you sure he doesn't just need TLC?'

Andrew's door opened at that moment, so Jess didn't bother to answer. Lucy followed her into the consulting room and closed the door behind them.

Jess explained about Russell. 'I'd like your opinion. I think he might be an acute appendix.'

Andrew frowned. 'I'll take a look—but, you know, Jess, we do get a lot of gastroenteritis amongst the students—especially the new ones. Most of it is food-related.'

Jess knew he was insinuating that she was panicking unnecessarily, especially when he went on to warn her, 'If you ask me to see every stomach upset that comes our way, the work of the centre will grind to a halt.'

CHAPTER THREE

COMPRESSING her lips, Jess kept her own counsel until she saw what Andrew thought of Russell.

She was pleased when, after taking a history and examining Russell's abdomen, he lifted an apologetic eyebrow towards her as he asked for gloves and jelly to carry out a much more intimate examination. 'This isn't very comfortable,' Andrew warned him, 'but I'm being as gentle as I can.'

Eventually straightening, he stripped off his gloves before saying, 'I think the nurse's suspicions might be right. I believe you have an inflamed appendix, Russell. You know what that means?'

The youth nodded. 'An operation?'

'Not necessarily,' Andrew reassured him. 'It may settle down with rest, but you need to be seen by a consultant, who will make the decision. I'll go and make a couple of telephone calls.'

Jess remained behind. While Russell dressed, she cleared away the debris. When he started to climb from the examination couch, she told him, 'I should stay there for the time being.'

Andrew was soon back, with Lucy in tow. 'Sister Robart is going to run you down to the local hospital in her car, Russell. The accident and emergency department. You'll be seen by the surgeons there.'

When Lucy had left with her charge, Andrew turned to Jess. 'Can you manage to hold the fort while she's away?'

Jess nodded, trying hard not to feel smug about being right.

Andrew, however, was professional enough to admit

he'd been wrong to say what he had. 'I take it all back. Well done.'

Raising her head, she discovered an unexpected approval in his expression that revived the fluttering in the pit of her stomach she'd experienced the day before.

Finding his presence unsettling, relief flooded through her when he made his way back to his consulting room. But she set about seeing the remainder of her patients with renewed enthusiasm.

What was left of the morning whizzed by without even time for a snatched coffee, so when she had dealt with the last patient, she sank gratefully onto the empty chair in the office.

'Thank goodness that's the lot. How's Russell?' she asked Lucy, who had returned some half-hour earlier and was catching up on the paperwork.

'They've admitted him for observation.' Her reply was curt and Jess guessed it was because she'd been right in her diagnosis.

'I wasn't certain it was appendicitis, Lucy, even though I've probably seen a lot more aching stomachs than you have. Initially, *I* jumped to the conclusion that it was the curry, but some sixth sense told me there was something not quite right.'

'Are you experienced in counselling as well?' Lucy's blunt query startled Jess.

'Counselling? Not really, only as far as it comes into a practice nurse's work.'

Lucy sniffed disdainfully. 'Andrew seems to think you have a flair for it. Said it was a good idea for me to leave it all to you.'

Sensing Lucy's hurt at this thoughtless remark, Jess began to feel quite sorry for the girl. Didn't the insufferable man appreciate that all these skills came with practice?

'Don't take it to heart. Men go for anything new, but soon tire of it.'

Lucy dragged out the words in her reply until they were

almost a whine. 'I certainly hope so—and that the novelty of you having a daughter wears off as well.'

Colouring hotly, Jess protested, 'My daughter? He's never met her.'

'No, but he likes her name. He said so.'

Lost for an answer, Jess was thankful that the surgery door opened at that moment and Andrew's last patient left.

'Are you going to the canteen, Lucy?' His question couldn't have been more inappropriate under the circumstances.

'I suppose I might as well. Perhaps by the time I return you'll have discovered everything there is to know about one another, and then we can get down to some proper work.'

Picking up her shoulder bag, she marched through the waiting area and slammed the outer door with sufficient force to set the panelled walls aquiver.

Horrified, Jess wished herself anywhere but in the one seat in the office that was in Andrew's view.

He was the first to speak.

'What brought on that little outburst?'

Jess hesitated before replying. 'I guess it was my being right about Russell—together with your suggestion that she left all the counselling to me.'

'Why?' Andrew seemed genuinely baffled. 'She hates the job.'

Jess smiled ruefully. 'That's immaterial—she saw your suggestion as a criticism of her work.'

Andrew threw up his hands in despair. 'And I thought I was doing her a good turn.'

'Coffee?' Jess thought it best to change the subject.

'Yes, please. It's been a long morning. I intended asking Lucy to bring me a sandwich back with her for once, but she didn't give me a chance.'

Jess laughed. 'Just as well. It would probably have been laced with arsenic. You're welcome to one of mine.' She proffered her box, containing a round of cheese and tomato sandwiches towards him.

'I can't take the food from your mouth. I'll wander down to the canteen myself.'

'It's up to you, but I rarely eat both of them.'

'You're sure?' Andrew asked, before helping himself to the one nearest him.

'Certain.'

He consumed it with obvious relish and murmured, 'That was delicious, thanks. Perhaps I ought to get up a bit earlier and make myself some lunch.'

Jess was thoughtful as she made the coffee. Was he implying he lived alone? That could explain Lucy's behaviour. If she was angling to become the future Mrs Brent it was no wonder Andrew's critical comment had upset her so badly.

She also puzzled over Lucy's remark that Andrew was smitten by Ruth, although she had to admit he'd appeared to have been thinking about the child when he'd told Jess not to rush in on the dot of nine.

'Has Lucy worked here long?' she asked as she handed him the coffee, being careful this time not to allow their fingers to touch.

Andrew thought for a moment. 'Nearly two years. We work well together.'

'What about the other girl, who has gone to look after her father?' Jess enquired.

'She was very young. Newly qualified, in fact. She's a lovely girl but I think we did her a disservice. She needed more experience before taking on a job like this.'

At Jess's frown he hastened to reassure her. 'That's why I was so relieved when the agency produced someone with your record.'

'You mean someone as old as I am,' she joshed, to hide her pleasure at having made some inroad into his prejudices.

'Mature, rather than old, I'd call it,' he grinned.

When she didn't respond immediately, he asked thoughtfully, 'I suppose you wouldn't be interested in applying for the advertised post?'

Although flattered by his suggestion, Jess shook her head. 'I'm better staying with the agency, at least until Ruth's older.'

'Why? You're obviously happy about her care while you're working here. Why not on a more regular basis?'

'It's all right when she's at school, but it's unfair not to be there to help out when she's ill.'

He frowned. 'Childhood illnesses are usually pretty mild these days.'

Jess shrugged. 'I know, but she's an asthmatic.'

'Bad?'

'Fortunately not. Controlled with an inhaler.'

'I see.' Andrew rose from his seat and came to stand by her desk, where he asked the question that had obviously been puzzling him since the day before. 'I *did* get the right impression, did I? It's her paternal grandparents looking after her?'

Wishing he would return to his own room, Jess nodded.

'That's unusual, isn't it?'

Realising he wasn't going to be satisfied with anything less than a full explanation, Jess sighed before giving him the facts briefly. 'Her father died. His parents hadn't wanted their only son to marry while still a student, so we lived together.'

Andrew's compassion was evident in the unashamed curiosity of his gaze. 'I guess losing her father didn't help Ruth's asthma any?'

'She doesn't remember him.' Jess was reluctant to say more, but he was waiting expectantly. 'I was living with *my* parents by that time.' She didn't add that she'd moved in with them in a fit of pique at Larry's appearing to care more about Bangladeshi refugees than his pregnant partner.

'So how come you live with his parents now?'

'I contacted them when I realised how they must feel, having lost their only son. I've very fond of them.'

His tentative pat on her shoulder, to signal his empathy, sent a shivering excitement scudding through her veins that made her grateful when he withdrew to his room.

Even though he could have no idea how his lightest of touches had burned deep into her consciousness, Jess needed time to regain her composure as she recognised he was not the uncaring person she had believed.

His interest in Ruth proved that. He didn't know the girl and yet his concern about her welfare was clearly genuine.

As she wondered again what had made him so distrustful of agency nurses, Lucy returned.

'Nothing to do then?' She asked. 'Aren't you the lucky one, Jess? If I remain here I get nothing but interruptions.' Her tone suggested she had turned away whatever work had arisen.

'We haven't been disturbed once.' Jess tried to defuse Lucy's antagonism. 'I think the students must all be waiting for your return.'

Jess had meant the comment sarcastically, so was astonished when Lucy treated it as a compliment.

'That's not surprising. They're used to me.'

Jess did her best to hide her amusement as she enquired, 'Coffee or tea? I could do with a refill.'

'Did Sylvia pop in, Andrew?' asked Lucy. 'She wants to know what time for squash this evening.'

Andrew frowned. 'I thought it was all arranged.'

Lucy shrugged. 'Perhaps I misunderstood. We met up in the canteen queue.'

Andrew sighed. 'I'd better ring her and check.'

He closed the door between the two rooms.

After she had made the coffee, Jess asked nonchalantly, 'Who's Sylvia?'

Lucy smiled maliciously. 'Andrew hasn't told you about the stunning librarian he used to live with?'

At Jess's shake of the head she continued, 'She's blonde,

she's beautiful, and oh, so brainy. The perfect match for our Dr Brent—especially as she's brilliant at sport as well.'

Jess felt an unexpected stab of jealousy. '*Used* to live with, you say?'

'That's right.' Lucy appeared not displeased at the thought. 'She used to work on this site but is now at Roundings. She comes over here for meetings, though, and when she does they meet up.'

'So why did she move out?'

Lucy shrugged. 'I don't really know. Perhaps she wanted to be nearer her work. Andrew wasn't best pleased at the time, I can tell you, but he seems to have accepted it now.'

'I see.' Although longing to learn more, Jess thought it prudent not to appear too curious and changed the subject. 'If you don't have to visit another site today, what is there to be done this afternoon?'

'Don't worry about being underemployed,' Lucy assured her sharply. 'There will be plenty of students to register. While you get on with that, I have the books to bring up-to-date.'

The waiting area was already filling with students eager to ensure there was somewhere for them to turn should illness strike. Jess grabbed a handful of forms and joined them, explaining the set-up, and this time suggesting they complete the forms immediately.

When the first batch of forms ran out, she turned for a further supply to find Andrew waiting to speak to her.

'Lucy and I could run a health-check on some of these today, provided they can spare ten minutes or so. Could you organise that for us, Jess?'

'No problem.' Jess went off to do as he suggested, and each time she handed him a list of names he nodded appreciatively.

So she was surprised when, as it approached five, he snapped, 'Steady on, Jess. That's quite enough for one day. Make appointments for anyone who has their timetable and then lock the door. I want to get away at five tonight.'

Of course. He was off to play squash with Sylvia and he didn't want to be late. When a shaft of jealousy made Jess catch her breath, she told herself it was because he would make Sylvia such a good husband and father while she had to manage alone.

To hide her feelings, she tidied the waiting room and office. The moment the others came through from the treatment area she said, 'If there's nothing else, I'll be off out of your way.'

Andrew looked at her sharply. 'You'll be here at nine tomorrow, won't you?'

'If that's when you need me.' Determined to continue trying to prove that agency nurses were not idlers, she added rashly, 'I can come earlier if it'll help.'

Raising his head, Andrew answered quickly, 'That won't be necessary.'

'Nine it is, then.'

After two days at the centre Jess knew more or less what was expected of her, and so Wednesday morning was much easier—especially as both Lucy and Andrew appeared to have accepted she knew what she was doing.

Having seen the last patient of the morning, Jess was chatting to Lucy when Andrew opened his door. 'I just rang the hospital. Russell had his appendix removed yesterday evening and is doing fine. Apparently he was pretty near perforating. It certainly wasn't the curry,' he chuckled.

Pleased to discover she'd been right, Jess made her way through to switch on the kettle and Andrew followed her. He closed the door behind him, leaving Lucy to deal with whoever had just come into the waiting area.

'I wondered if you'd like to come with me to visit Ian this afternoon?'

'You know what's wrong, then?' Jess asked eagerly.

'Cagey, as usual, the lab won't commit themselves until they've done more tests. I must check how he's coping, though, and let him know about the delay.'

'If it'll help, I'll call in on my way home and see if there's anything I can do for him,' Jess offered.

'We'll go together, but in separate cars, then you can go straight on home.'

'Sounds OK to me. If Lucy doesn't need me here, that is.'

At the mention of her name, Lucy uncannily materialised in the doorway.

'There's a student here I think you ought to see, Andrew. Could be a nasty does of glandular fever.' Her eyes swivelled from one to the other, and Jess guessed it was because she'd heard her name mentioned.

Andrew took the student through to his consulting room and Jess was about to explain what she'd been saying when the waiting area began to fill with students wanting to register. 'I'll see to these,' she murmured.

Lucy didn't reply, and Jess knew she still had a long way to go before Lucy trusted her completely.

Twenty minutes later, she heard Andrew emerge from the consulting room, and she turned to see him smiling towards Lucy. 'Mike's not feeling too great at the moment, are you?' he asked as the student followed him from the consulting room. 'I think it would be safer if you accompany him back to his room. He's in the halls. Nant Block, isn't it, Mike?'

The student nodded, and Lucy, who could do nothing but agree, took his arm and helped him from the room. 'I'll call in the canteen on my way back,' she said.

Jess left the new students to fill in their personal details and joined Andrew in the office.

'Is it glandular fever?'

'Pretty certainly, but I've taken blood for confirmation. There's not a lot else we can do. The fever just has to take its course.

Jess nodded. 'When you said "the halls", did you mean the two four-storeyed blocks just after the entrance?'

Andrew nodded. 'They are the accommodation blocks

that were originally built. The newer rooms are much more student-friendly.'

'And they are where?'

'Just across that field, opposite our entrance. They're not big blocks, but more like houses, with ten rooms each, and they actually have a bit of character. But, due to the usual lack of finance, there are only a few. I don't know how or when the rest will be built.'

When the newly registered students eventually left, Andrew had made coffee for them both, so Jess offered him half her lunch as she had the day before.

He pulled Lucy's chair up opposite Jess, which allowed his gaze to slide slowly over her face. 'This is delicious.'

Embarrassed by his scrutiny, Jess shrugged. 'You're welcome.'

'Which is more than *you* were on Monday.' He dropped his gaze and took one of her hands. 'I'm afraid we were guilty of generalising. It won't happen again, I promise.'

Disconcerted by his touch again initiating a surging warmth, Jess freed her hand and, to hide her confusion, said reproachfully, 'I should hope not.'

She was saved by another batch of students wanting to register. Lucy was back by the time she had dealt with them, so Andrew suggested they set out on their visit.

Ian was feeling better for his rest, and even doing some studying. 'Perhaps by the time you get the results I'll be cured,' he joked, although they all knew he was still far from well.

When Andrew had to leave to make another visit, Jess stayed and chatted to Ian, alleviating his worries about his lectures and reassuring him as far as she could about his health.

Before she left, she asked, 'Is there anything I can do or get for you while I'm here, Ian?'

He shook his head. 'A couple of friends have got in the shopping I need, thanks.'

Jess returned to her family after completing the rest of

her day's work conscious she had done well with Ian, and her optimistic mood continued into the next day.

'What can I do for you this morning?' She smiled warmly as she greeted the clearly nervous girl who was her first patient of the morning.

'I—I think… I think—' Tears had formed in the girl's eyes as she tried to bring herself to tell Jess what was worrying her.

Handing her a tissue, Jess prompted gently, 'What do you think, Natalie?'

'I think I'm pregnant.' This time the words exploded from the girl as if she could no longer keep them back.

'What makes you think so?' Jess had seated herself alongside the girl and now rested a hand on her shoulder.

'It was at the Freshers' Ball. I drank too much and don't really remember how it happened.'

Jess knew from student gossip that the Freshers' Ball had taken place the night before, so she found it difficult to keep the doubt from her voice as she asked, 'I was really more interested in why you *now* think you're pregnant?'

The girl looked up at her with terrified wide eyes. 'I was sick this morning, and I should have come on today, but there's no sign of it.'

Jess felt a rush of pity for the girl as she wondered what kind of parents could have let such an innocent come away to college without first enlightening her about the true facts of life.

'Natalie, you were probably only sick because you drank too much alcohol. And as for being half a day late, it often happens when girls move away from home for the first time. It can be weeks before things get back to normal. There's always a chance of an unplanned pregnancy under these circumstances, but the morning after is far too early for any signs to develop.'

'Are you sure?' The terrified fresher's eyes begged for reassurance.

'I'm very sure.' Jess gave the answer the student was looking for.

After digesting it thoughtfully, she asked timidly, 'If I was pregnant, when would I know?'

'We could do a test when your period is a couple of weeks overdue, but even then the rest would not be a certainty. However, in cases like yours, the doctor can prescribe what's known as the ''morning-after pill'' for you. That'll ensure there's no pregnancy.'

'Is—is that safe?' Natalie's eyes were wide with terror.

'Reasonably, in a healthy person, but it's for use only in an emergency. It means you will be taking an extremely high dose of the contraceptive pill within just twelve hours.'

Tears welled up in the student's eyes again. 'Do I *have* to take it?'

'No. It's your choice, once you know all the facts. At the moment you're in no position to decide, and we need to remedy that.'

Gently, trying not to worry the girl further, she broached the subjects of contraception, pregnancy and the need for safe sex. When she felt Natalie understood all she had said so far, she produced a booklet that explained the use of condoms to prevent unwanted pregnancies as well as the transmission of disease.

The girl's eyes brightened at the sight of it. 'We used one of those, because of AIDS.'

Breathing a heartfelt sigh of relief, Jess replied, 'In that case you really have very little chance of being pregnant. The condom prevents pregnancy as well as the passage of disease. Together with the fact you're not at the most fertile part of your cycle, I'd say it's unnecessary to take the pills.'

'You guarantee I won't be pregnant?'

'No one can ever do that, Natalie. No method of contraception is infallible. Even the morning-after pill has its failures. Nothing is one hundred per cent safe. That's why it's so important to think hard and long and be sure you know

what you're doing. Sex can be much more beautiful in a
meaningful relationship. It's worth waiting for.'

'I can see that now.' Natalie sniffed. 'I never intended—
Oh, I wish I hadn't been so stupid. I didn't know the wine
would affect me in that way.'

Jess felt desperately sorry for the girl, and said gently,
'Well, taking all the circumstances into account, it's most
unlikely you are pregnant. However, you have to be happy
with any decision you make.'

Her words were greeted by a renewed outburst of sobbing. 'I don't know—I don't want to take the tablets, but
if I don't and I'm pregnant—' She paused dramatically. 'I'll
kill myself.'

Jess placed an arm around the girl. 'You know, it's not
the end of the world to be pregnant.'

'It is when I'm not married.' Natalie was scandalised.

'Neither was I, but I survived to tell the tale.'

Natalie received the confession with open amazement.
'What did you do?'

'Carried on with my life and in due course had a baby
girl who now brings me enormous happiness.' Jess knew
she was twisting the facts slightly, but the girl needed every
ounce of reassurance Jess could muster if she was to enjoy
her first taste of independence.

'My mother would never forgive me.' Natalie was still
far from convinced.

'You think so now, but I guarantee you'd be surprised.
I was. Mine was wonderfully supportive, as I'm sure yours
would be if you were in trouble.'

Natalie shook her head. 'I don't know about that.'

Jess wasn't sure either. A mother who was unable to tell
her daughter the facts of life, even when she was leaving
home, was unlikely to be easy to talk to. However, there
was no problem pregnancy at the moment, only a decision
to make that Natalie must be happy with.

Conscious that she had a long list of patients waiting to
be seen, Jess now sought to bring the interview to a close.

'I'll give you some booklets to take away and study, Natalie. They'll give you a much clearer understanding of the whole subject. If you should change your mind later today, or tomorrow, there'll still be time for you to take the pills. If there's anything you don't understand, come and chat with either the doctor or myself. In any case, I'd like you to come and see me again tomorrow—just to let me know how you're getting on.'

Her fears partly resolved, the student left, leaving Jess exhausted but satisfied.

The next few patients' problems were quickly sorted, without Jess expounding too much concentration. Nevertheless, by mid-morning she felt in need of a quick break.

Discovering the other two were busy, she made just the one coffee and sat down to complete the paperwork for her last consultation.

Andrew came in at that moment, closing the door behind him. Eyeing the steaming mug, he murmured, 'Don't I get one?'

Flustered, Jess stood up, intending to switch the kettle on again. But he was too quick for her. Resting a hand lightly on her shoulder, he guided her back down to her seat. 'Sit down. You probably need to.'

'I certainly do.' To cover her confusion, she hastened to tell him why. 'My first case this morning drained me of all the energy I possessed.'

'What was that?'

'A terrified fresher so naïve it was hard to believe in this day and age.'

Andrew sighed as he straddled the other chair. 'Not as uncommon as you might think. What was this one's problem? Sex, alcohol, drugs or—?'

'Just the first two, thank goodness. I don't think I could have coped with anything more.'

He grinned. 'She got drunk at the Freshers' Ball and a

wicked male took advantage of her. I know. I hear it every year—at least once!'

'This one didn't complain about the other half of the equation. She seemed to consider the guilt was all hers.'

He laughed. 'Times *must* be a-changing. Women's Lib on the wane, is it?'

Jess gave him a straight look. 'I wouldn't know anything about that.'

Laughing again, he made himself a coffee, before re-calling he was there for a reason.

'Jess—I've just seen a third-year student who I think you might be able to help. Melissa's married, and expecting her first baby just before Christmas, but she still wants to sit her finals next summer. She's back out in the waiting room.'

'There are quite a few ahead of her to be seen,' Jess said, but, pleased that he considered she could help, she suggested, 'Perhaps it would be better to arrange for her to come back later?'

He handed her the girl's records. 'Whatever you think best. But she's going home at lunchtime and won't be back until Monday. You'll still be with us then?'

'I—er—I haven't decided.'

He searched her face intently. 'You haven't another commitment?'

She shook her head. 'No, but—'

'That's settled, then. I'd like you to stay—at least another week.'

Jess met his gaze with a surprised start. 'I'll have to check with the agency.'

'You do that. The moment you're finished this morning.'

Expecting a mini-riot if she called in the mother-to-be before the other waiting patients, she went out into the waiting room to chat to the girl.

All the time she was making an appointment to see the student the following week she felt quietly satisfied that, after only four days, Andrew thought enough of her work to want her to stay on.

Returning to the treatment room, she dealt with the remaining patients quickly and efficiently.

When she rang them, the agency agreed to her staying as long as she was required there, and Jess began to feel more settled.

As she saw her last patient on Friday morning, Jess wondered what had happened to Natalie. She guessed she would have to ask Andrew's advice about chasing her up.

Lucy had just gone to lunch, however, when the door to the waiting room opened and Jess looked up to see the girl. 'Come through to the treatment room,' she told her, as Natalie started to speak. 'It's more confidential in here.'

'I've come, like you said. I'm sorry I missed surgery.'

'It doesn't matter,' Jess assured her.

'I—I've read all the booklets, and thought about it, and I really don't want to take the pills.' She finished in a rush, her cheeks burning with a fiery glow.

'That's fine by me, as long as you're happy about it.'

'You think I'm right, don't you?' the student asked anxiously. 'I mean, you agree there really is no danger?'

'Like I said yesterday, I can't give an absolute guarantee. If you're not happy with your decision, why don't you have a chat with the doctor? He's got his last patient with him at the moment.'

'No. I'd rather not. I've made up my mind.' Natalie sprang from the chair. 'Thanks anyway.'

'One thing before you go. I don't suppose anyone has ever discussed cervical smear tests with you, have they?'

'Smear? No—I—'

'You don't need one until you're been sexually active for a year. I presume the other night was your first time?'

Her eyes wide, Natalie nodded. 'Will I need one after just that once? I'm only eighteen.'

'It's important to have them regularly, however young you are. Do you know why we do them?'

'To look for cancer?'

'Not cancer itself, just early signs that might mean the disease would develop in the future. Worth remembering, though, don't you think?'

'I couldn't face the doctor.'

'You don't have to see the doctor. One of us can do it.' Jess handed her a leaflet on the subject and urged her to read it and not forget when the right time came.

The girl nodded. 'I won't. I promise.'

'I wonder,' Jess mused as the door banged behind Natalie.

She was still completing her paperwork when Andrew's patient also left, so she switched on the kettle, knowing she couldn't but offer him some lunch as usual.

'Who was that banging the door?' He took the proffered sandwich from Jess. 'Did you have a problem?'

'No, it was the naïve girl I mentioned yesterday. She's decided not to take the morning-after pill and was trying to escape from my clutches.'

'You should have let me talk with her,' he remonstrated.

'Why?'

'Because I'm the one who'll have to deal with the consequences,' he retorted hotly.

'What consequences?'

'Pregnancy, of course.' He was angry now.

'You still don't trust me, do you?' She glared at him. 'For your information, her partner wore a condom and it was the day before her period was due. Would you have risked giving her a hefty dose of contraceptive hormones under those circumstances?'

'Well, no. But if she herself doesn't accept there's not much risk—'

'Andrew, I'm not a fool. I gave Natalie all the information, both verbal and written, that she needed to make up her own mind, and she thought about it for twenty-four hours. On balance, she's happier not taking the pills.'

'So why the banged door?'

Jess gave him a wry smile. 'Because I told her about the need for a cervical smear test in the future. I guessed it might be my only opportunity. She couldn't get away quickly enough!'

CHAPTER FOUR

'I SEE.' A smile accompanied his words—Andrew was hoping to make amends for his tetchiness—but it clearly had no effect.

His heart sank as he watched a look of disdain cross her face, and he knew he deserved it. He'd bawled her out again. And for no good reason except that when he'd first started in practice an agency nurse had failed to diagnose a pregnant woman. A mistake which had nearly cost him his reputation.

They weren't all alike and Jess was proof of that. He couldn't have done anything more for Natalie than Jess had, but that experience had left its mark, and here he was taking it out on Jess.

Leaning against the doorjamb, he watched her make the coffee. 'After we finish at Roundings, Lucy and I will call on Ian. Before we go, Jess, I thought you might like to have a look at his results. I'm afraid it's as I thought. Kidneys definitely not working properly. I'll have to let him know and get him to a specialist as soon as possible to find out why.'

'Poor Ian. Can he continue his studies?'

'I should think once they get him sorted out he'll have more energy than he's had for many months. I hope so, anyway.'

When they'd left, Jess appreciated being on her own. She thought about her decision to return the following week, and, though she was tempted to change her mind after his earlier outburst, she decided the hours were so convenient that she would put up with his hassle for a few more days.

* * *

Ruth was up early on Saturday morning, so Jess dressed them both for a relaxing time in the garden.

After breakfast, however, Gwen asked Jess, 'Would you mind popping down to the supermarket?'

'Not at all. What do you want?'

When Gwen gave her the list, Jess saw it was only a couple of items, and so slipped an enormous sweatshirt over her tracksuit bottoms and drove Ruth down to the shopping precinct and parked the car.

As they wandered round the aisles Jess was concentrating on the shelves, searching for the items Gwen required, and so didn't notice anyone until her way was barred by another trolley.

She looked up, and her eyes were caught and held by Andrew's. Noting how smart he looked, in light casual trousers and rugby-type shirt, Jess was embarrassed that she hadn't bothered to change them both into tidier clothes. She stuttered, 'Sorry. I—er—I—what are you doing here?'

'The same as you,' he laughed. 'My cupboard is bare.'

'Oh!'

Jess was lost for words as he crouched down and spoke to Ruth. 'You helping Mummy today?'

Ruth nodded. 'Who are you?' she asked.

'My name is Andrew. Your mummy has been working with me this week.'

'I like you 'cos you let her come home at teatime.'

He looked up towards Jess. 'Would you like a coffee and a fruit juice or something?'

Ruth squealed, 'Oohem-yes, please.' But Jess shook her head.

'We only popped in for a couple of items.'

Ruth took his hand and, pulling him up, started to drag him towards the coffee shop. 'I'd like a drink. It's horrid, you know, when Mummy isn't home at my bedtime.'

He grinned and winked at Jess. 'Seems like you're over-ruled.'

Sure he had deliberately made the suggestion in Ruth's

hearing so that Jess couldn't refuse, she felt her cheeks flame. She wanted to keep their relationship strictly a working one. She and Ruth were doing very nicely on their own, and that was the way she wanted it to continue.

So, while he ordered the coffees and an orange squash for Ruth, she told the little girl, 'He's a very busy man. You mustn't bother him, otherwise he won't let me work with him any more.'

When he joined them with the tray of drinks, he tried every way to draw Ruth out to talk to him again, but she answered only briefly.

He frowned as he drank his coffee and Jess knew he was puzzled by the change in the little girl. The moment Ruth had drained her glass, Jess pushed back her chair and, rising to her feet, said, 'We have to go now. Thanks for the refreshment.'

His penetrating look left Jess weak as she made her way back to her trolley, and on to the checkout, all the while wondering why he'd taken such an interest in another man's child.

She wasn't surprised, either, when over their lunchtime sandwich on Monday, he asked, 'What did you say to your daughter that made her stop talking to me?'

'I told her you were a busy man.'

'Is that all? I could have sworn you'd warned her not to talk to me.'

Jess tried futilely to prevent a guilty blush staining her cheeks.

'She's a little charmer, isn't she? I was enjoying our chat.'

Jess shrugged and changed the subject. 'Are you and Lucy going to Roundings this afternoon?'

'No. You are coming with me.'

'But…'

'Don't argue. I'd like to hear more about Ruth.'

'I'm afraid I can't come with you. I've arranged to see Melissa.' Jess was relieved to have a sound excuse not to go with him. She wasn't prepared to share Ruth with anyone.

When they had left for Roundings, Jess saw it was nearly time for her appointment with the pregnant student.

'Hi, Melissa, come through. I'm Jess.' She closed the door she had been holding open for the mother-to-be.

'Call me Mel. It's good of you to give up your time to see me like this. I gather you have a little girl? Dr Brent seemed to think you manage to balance your time between work, home and parenthood very successfully, so you might be able to give me some hints.'

Surprised to hear he'd been so complimentary, when he knew next to nothing about them, Jess asked, 'Have you a particular problem?'

'I don't think so.'

'What does your husband do?'

'He graduated last year and is working for an accountancy firm in Bradstoke.'

'So he'll be able to help with the baby?'

'Mmm,' Melissa seemed dubious. 'He's working for more exams and it takes up most of his spare time. That's what worries me most. I feel I've got the easy option, being able to study full-time, but even so…'

'Even so, you're going to need some form of childcare,' Jess finished for her.

'I'm hoping my mum will help out.'

'She lives nearby?'

'No, but she's a widow and isn't working at the moment, so could come and stay when I need her. But that could cause problems with Paul.'

'When are your finals?'

'May.'

'So the baby will be five to six months old then?' Jess said thoughtfully. 'Apart from when you need to attend lectures, you should hopefully soon settle into a routine that will allow you to study while the baby sleeps. Have you checked out the crèche here?'

Mel nodded. 'They don't take young babies.'

'Working as I do, for an agency, I have lots of contacts in the area. I'll see if I can find someone reliable to help you out when you have to be in college.'

'That's kind of you.' Mel hesitated. 'I suppose…I suppose *you* wouldn't be willing to take it on? I mean, we'll pay you, and it would mean you would be home with your own little girl.'

Jess smiled. 'I'm not sure it would work. You see, I have to earn enough to keep my daughter. Her father is dead.'

Mel's cheeks coloured prettily as she clapped a hand to her mouth. 'I'm sorry. I'd no idea.'

'No reason why you should. Leave this with me, and I'll see what I can find out. There's plenty of time before you need to make a decision.'

They went on to discuss Mel's antenatal care and several other minor problems, many of which Jess felt she'd resolved for the girl by the end of their chat.

As Jess showed her out she said, 'Keep in touch. I'll see what I can find out, and if I'm not still working here, I'll leave the details with Dr Brent. OK?'

Mel looked disappointed. 'I might not see you again, then? I should have realised you wouldn't be here long, being from an agency.'

Jess laughed. 'Sorry about that, but there'll always be someone here to chat with, even if it's not me.'

'But they might not have known the problems, like you.'

Jess returned to her paperwork with a heavy heart. She enjoyed working with the students, but she wasn't sure that Lucy would want her to continue here permanently, or that Andrew would ever trust her work completely if she did stay.

When Andrew and Lucy returned, Jess had completed her notes and the desk was tidy.

'How did you get on with Mel?' he asked.

'Fine. I've offered to try and find out about childcare for when she's at lectures.'

'I thought you were going to say you'd offered to do it yourself.'

Jess laughed. 'Funnily enough, she did suggest that, but I declined.'

He frowned. 'I would have thought it could be the ideal solution for you and Ruth.'

'Maybe, But I have to earn my keep.'

'Pity.' He appeared to do some hard thinking, but obviously found no solution. Instead he turned to smile at her warmly. 'Thanks anyway. I think that's all Mel needs. Support from someone who's been through it.'

He checked his watch. 'Hey, it's after five. Don't let us keep you, Jess. At this time your daughter needs you more than we do. Go on,' he urged as she hesitated, looking in Lucy's direction. 'Scoot.'

Although Jess was warmed again by his continuing concern for Ruth's welfare, it made her wish that Larry was still alive and able to care in a similar way.

She didn't understand why, but it was a relief to escape Andrew's interest. For someone still involved with his previous live-in girlfriend, he seemed to be far too concerned about her life with Ruth.

The little girl had just settled on Tuesday evening when the telephone's peremptory buzz broke in on Jess's thoughts. 'I'll get it.' After their day of caring for her daughter, she strove to make the evenings restful for Gwen and Les. She hurried out to the hall and lifted the receiver.

'Is that Jess Fenn?'

'Ye-es.'

'My name's Rachel Mull. I'm the warden for the Roundings site halls. Dr Brent asked me to ring you and ask if you can possibly give us a hand.'

'In what way?'

'We have a fire in one wing of the halls. We think everyone is accounted for, but even so, many of the uninjured students are hysterical.' Her voice, which had started the explanation calmly, began to rise to a pitch that made Jess wonder if the warden wasn't far from hysteria herself.

'There are so many needing attention that Dr Brent and Sister Robart just can't see them quickly enough, and obviously the sooner we get them settled down, the less traumatic it'll be.'

Sensing it would be better to leave any questions until she arrived at the site, Jess assured her, 'I'll be over as soon as I can.'

Jess hated leaving Gwen and Les again, but felt her absence was justified under the circumstances.

She explained the situation as quickly as she could. 'Ruth's sound asleep and with any luck won't wake. I'll be back just as soon as I can.'

'Take your time. We're all right. You worry too much.' Gwen accompanied her to the door and watched her drive off.

Discovering one road approaching the site was blocked with cars and ghoulish onlookers, and the other cordoned off by the emergency services, Jess parked her car as near as she could and completed the journey on foot. As she entered the gates she was confronted by a milling mass of students, all seeming uncertain what to do next.

Spotting a fireman approaching, she rushed over and enquired if they knew where Dr Brent was.

'You the reinforcements, love? Great. He's on the ground floor, through that door. He'll be glad to see you.'

Just completing his examination of the smoke-affected eyes of a couple of students, Andrew greeted her warmly.

'The injured have mostly gone to hospital already, but I think these two could do with a check-up. Whistle one of those ambulancemen over for me, would you? And ask if they have a supply of eye pads.'

Jess returned with a couple of paramedics ready for action. 'You wanted eye pads, Doctor?' One of the men handed a box over.

Taping pads over the eyes he'd just finished examining,

Andrew indicated Jess should cover the eyes of the girl nearest her.

'This is just a precaution,' he reassured them both. 'In case the heat and smoke have done more damage than I can detect in this light.'

He turned to the ambulance driver. 'These two to the eye hospital, please. And don't leave them alone for a moment,' he ordered the other paramedic.

He looked at Jess, and a ghost of a smile briefly crossed his lips. 'I hope you've brought lots of patience and TLC, because that's what's needed now. Could you go and chat to that group of students over there?'

Noting the exhaustion haunting his eyes, Jess resisted the almost overwhelming temptation to wipe his brow clean of the grime that clung there, and nodded willingly.

She moved along the corridor to join a group of six tearful young girls. She led them further along and sat them on the floor. 'First of all, is anyone hurt?'

They all shook their heads, and an older girl assumed the role of spokeswoman. 'Gen jumped from her window. She was Eleanor's friend.' She indicated a girl still sobbing violently. 'No one seems to know how she is and she was rushed off in the ambulance before any of us could see her.'

'In that case she's in the best hands, isn't she?' Jess's calm reasoning began to have an effect. Looking around, she found most of the girls nodding. 'I can assure you in situations like this the emergency services don't waste time and resources on hopeless cases. I know it's awful, not knowing anything definite, but you'd rather the hospital staff concentrate their efforts on looking after your friends than answering the phone to your enquiries, wouldn't you?'

When Jess saw all the girls agreed with the logic of what she was saying, and had begun to come to terms with their own fears, she moved on to chat to others exhibiting similar signs of distress.

Andrew was doing the same, until he found a young girl

crouched in a dark corner. Her eyes were tightly shut against the pain of a severe burn on her left palm.

'Come over here and give me a hand, Jess,' he called, whilst in the same breath he murmured soothingly to the victim, 'What happened?'

The girl opened one eye, flinching as Andrew gently attempted to examine the injury. 'I—I—' Her voice broke as floods of tears were unleashed. 'It was my engagement ring. I went back for it.'

'Where's the ring now?' he asked quietly as he carefully attempted to uncurl her fingers.

'In my pocket.' The girl sniffed, before managing a weak smile through watery eyes.

'So all we have to worry about is getting your hand better so you can wear it again?'

As the floodgates reopened, allowing tears to stream down her cheeks, Jess took her other hand and asked quietly, 'What's your name?'

'Zoe. Zoe Berwick.' She tried to control her sobs.

'Well, Zoe, I know it hurts like hell at the moment, but I don't think there's any permanent damage.' He turned to Jess. 'Is there any Flamazine in my bag over there?'

Jess searched quickly. 'I can't see any, but you have a pack of Jelonet.'

'We won't use that today. Just cover it with a dry dressing until she gets to hospital.'

Jess brought one over and at Andrew's nod fixed it gently in place.

While Jess was occupied, he searched for, and found, a couple of painkilling tablets in his bag. 'These should help the pain, Zoe. Can you swallow them without water?' She nodded eagerly as Andrew wrote down the treatment he had given and handed the note to the driver of an ambulance for seated patients standing by. 'Can you find her a drink before you set off?'

The driver nodded. 'No problem. We carry water.'

'Good. See you later, then,' Andrew promised as Zoe

was led away. He smiled ruefully at Jess. 'I think it's back to the hysterical fray now.' He wiped the back of his hand across his brow, rubbing another streak of grimy sweat towards his hairline.

Smiling, Jess handed him a clean tissue, and when he didn't take it immediately she used it to clear the worst of the debris from his forehead.

As she lowered her hand, Andrew caught it in his own and raised a storm of emotion within her by kissing the back of her fingers. 'Thank you, kind lady,' he murmured, before turning to check on a couple of girls newly returned from the hospital.

When he was next free, he asked, 'Would you come with me to check on Maria—you remember, the von Recklinghausen's? She was a bit over-emotional so Rachel's taken her to a room in another part of the building. I want to check up on her, but I'd rather have a chaperon when I do. She's apparently complaining of jolting her back when she was hurrying from the fire.'

They found Maria lying on the bed sobbing.

As Jess closed the door of the room, Andrew took one of the girl's hands in his. 'Where does it hurt, Maria?'

She twisted slightly and pointed to her operation site.

As Andrew gently examined the area, he asked what had happened. 'I was running, and I turned round to see if Leonie was following me and my back seemed to lock.'

Andrew nodded, asked Maria to make several different movements of her limbs and then carried out a full neurological examination.

Eventually he sat down on the bed beside her. 'I don't think you've done any serious damage, Maria. You've probably strained some of the muscles in your back that aren't yet back to one hundred per cent efficiency.

'I'll give you a couple of tablets now, and I want you to stay there and rest. I'll be back to see you later.'

As they walked down the corridor from her room, he told Jess, 'Not surprisingly, she needs an awful lot of reassurance. But I do have to be careful. She tends to take any attention I give her the wrong way.'

And that wasn't surprising either, Jess thought. With his looks and caring bedside manner, he could charm the birds out of the trees if he wanted to. As she returned to her task of comforting the other students, she knew she was already far too aware of his attraction herself.

She had no idea how long she worked. Having removed her watch whilst bathing Ruth, and in her rush not retrieved it, she was startled when Andrew called to her, 'I think we're winning, but it's nearly midnight. I'll manage now if you're needed at home.'

Jess smiled. 'I shouldn't think so. If I can still be of help, I'll stay.' She looked around. 'Where's Lucy?'

He ambled across to join her. 'She followed the last bad lot to hospital. I told her to go on home from there.'

'When was that?'

'Not long before you arrived.' He regarded her warmly before saying quietly. 'The agency certainly knew what they were talking about when they recommended you for this job.'

To her fury, Jess felt her colour mounting. 'What do you mean?'

'The moment you arrived, the chaos and confusion—on which Lucy and I had been unable to make the slightest impression—disappeared like magic.' Raising an appraising eyebrow, he continued, 'You move amongst us exuding an air of contagious calm.'

Jess laughingly dismissed the extravagant compliment. 'I just arrived at the right time. You and Lucy had done the hard work earlier. You must be exhausted. It's *you* who ought to be getting off home.'

Andrew smiled and patted her shoulder. 'Nice of you to say so, but I'm staying put. Rachel has found me a room for the night, so, unless you want to share it, I should get back to your family.'

As he made the outrageous proposition, Jess had a

strange feeling that it wasn't meant as lightly as his tone suggested. Consequently her reply was sharper than she intended. 'In that case, I'll go. If the students don't need me, my family do.'

'OK. See you later this morning.'

Her professional commitment wouldn't allow her just to walk out. 'You're quite sure there's nothing else you want me to do?'

'I could think of many things, but, as they're not on offer, thank you very much for all you've done so far, Jess, and goodnight.'

Dismissing his comments as nothing more than his way of overcoming the tensions of the evening, she made her way contentedly back to her car.

When she arrived home she was pleased to find the house quiet and slipped gratefully into bed, where she slept soundly until woken by her alarm.

'You're surely not going to the surgery this morning?' Gwen enquired as Jess made her way to the breakfast table. 'You must be exhausted after last night. I'm sure the agency wouldn't expect you to.'

'I don't exactly feel refreshed, but neither will the others. We were all at the fire last night, Gwen, and I wouldn't be at all surprised if the doctor never made it to bed. I can't let them down.' Or give them a chance to say 'I told you so', she added silently.

'I see.' Gwen obviously didn't, but she knew better than to argue when Jess had made up her mind.

Jess left Ruth at the school gate at the usual time and was waiting at the surgery door when Andrew joined her.

He frowned. 'No Lucy?'

Assuming the obvious answer, he unlocked the door. 'Let's hope we're not busy this morning. I don't think I could cope.'

'Would a cup of coffee help?' Jess was already filling the kettle and Andrew smiled gratefully.

'You anticipate my every need.' He slumped into the chair behind his desk and groaned.

'What time did you get to bed—or didn't you?'

'It must have been after four—most of the students returned from hospital after treatment and it took time for them to settle. Thank goodness no one was seriously hurt.'

'What about the girl who jumped from the window?'

'Nothing more than a broken leg. Another couple were kept in with smoke inhalation, but they should all be out today.'

'Was Maria OK?'

He nodded. 'She slept from when we left her until Rachel and I looked in on her about four. Our reassurance must have done the trick.'

The waiting room door opened to admit a couple of patients and Andrew frowned again. 'This is not like Lucy. I would have thought we'd have heard from her if she wasn't coming in.'

'Perhaps she's just late. After all, you don't know what time she got away from the hospital last night. There could be all kinds of reasons.' She handed him the cup of coffee. 'I'll start booking them in and see how it goes.'

'Until Lucy arrives, tell all new registrations to come back when surgery's over. That'll cut the load a bit.'

Jess pasted up a notice to that effect and was surprised to find she could cope quite easily with the reception duties and seeing some of the patients. If she was in the treatment room, Andrew called his own patients through, and by the end of the surgery hours they were working well as a team.

As the last student left his consulting room, Andrew rubbed his eyes and yawned. 'Thank goodness that's the lot. Any more of that reviving coffee going spare?' he pleaded.

When Jess handed him the steaming mug, he motioned her towards the other chair in his room. 'Bring your coffee in here—the door's locked, isn't it? We deserve a respite.'

She accepted gratefully. As he sipped his coffee he

watched her thoughtfully, but he said nothing. When, having drained her mug, she stood up, intending to start on the new registrations, he held up a restraining hand. 'Sit down,' he told her. 'That was no way a long enough break.'

She did as he said, reluctantly. 'I'm all right. It's not long to lunchtime.'

He nodded. 'Still no word from Lucy? Perhaps I ought to ring her.'

As he dialled the number Jess moved away, unlocking the waiting room door to admit a surge of students to register.

By lunchtime, Jess was shattered and starving.

Having relocked the door, she took out her sandwich box.

'Put that away,' Andrew ordered. 'We're going out for some proper food today.'

'What if there's an emergency?'

'I'll have my radio-pager.'

'Did you speak to Lucy?'

Apparently baffled, he shook his head, 'No reply.'

His touch as he took her arm to help her into the Granada made Jess wish she hadn't agreed to go for the meal.

Telling herself it was nothing more than his way of saying thank you for all she'd done, she tried to relax.

'Where are we going?'

'Not far. A little place I know off the Cobbold Road. It doesn't get too crowded and the food is home cooked.'

The bistro was even smaller than Jess had anticipated, but everything about it gleamed.

'I'm sorry, Dr Brent. The only table we have free is by the kitchen. I hope that'll be all right.'

He nodded gratefully. 'My fault. I should have rung.'

The proprietor showed them to a table covered with red gingham that was spotlessly clean. The background music was muted and the scintillating aromas wafting towards them each time the kitchen door opened told Jess how much she was going to enjoy her lunch.

'You've obviously been here before?'

'Just occasionally—quite often, in fact. I don't enjoy cooking for myself.'

He didn't enlarge on his answer, but reached for the menu. 'What shall we have—the dish of the day?'

'What is it?'

'Navarin D'Agneau—or, in other words, lamb stew! I can highly recommend it.'

'Sounds fine.'

The waiter took their order, and enquired about wine.

Andrew looked inquiringly towards Jess, who shook her head. 'I'll be asleep across the desk if I do. Just water for me.'

'And me.' Andrew grinned.

The food arrived almost immediately. The lamb was exquisitely tender and the combination of vegetables and herbs in the dish brought out the flavour superbly. Jess thought she had never enjoyed a meal so much, and she had to admit it was partly due to the company.

She refused dessert. 'I couldn't.'

They both settled for coffee.

'So,' Andrew invited, his voice low, 'tell me about yourself.'

'I was born and educated in Worcestershire. Then I trained as a nurse here in Bradstoke—not too far from home, but not too close either. There's nothing more to tell.' She deliberately omitted any mention of Larry, and instead looked up at him from under veiled lashes. 'What about you?'

As she finished speaking his radio-pager bleeped.

'Damn.' He took it from his pocket, then frowned. 'It's the surgery number. I suppose Lucy must be there at long last. I'd better ring in and see if it's urgent.'

He didn't get through the first time, so he settled the bill and then tried again.

Lucy was clearly unhappy at having found the surgery empty. Jess listened as Andrew did his best to placate her and denied all knowledge of something she was accusing him of.

'We're coming back now anyway.' He replaced the receiver and with a puzzled expression led the way out to the car.

'What is it, Andrew? An emergency?'

He didn't speak until they were both settled in their seats and he had started up the engine. Even then he ignored her question and asked, 'When you arrived at the surgery this morning, was there a note attached to the door?'

Jess shook her head. 'As far as I remember it was bare.'

'Lucy said she rang in saying she was going straight to the hospital to take one of the students home. The porter who took the message says he pinned a note to the door.'

Jess frowned. 'That's very odd.'

'Very.' Andrew was pensive for a moment. 'Jess, Lucy is accusing you of removing it to get her into trouble. The pair of you haven't exactly hit it off.' He hesitated. 'You didn't, did you?'

That he even had to ask sent a cold hand clutching at her heart.

'You can't seriously believe that I, or anyone in our profession would be so petty?' An icy fury made her voice waver. 'Or could you?'

A sudden cold certainty told her that he did. Despite all Jess's efforts to prove herself to him, Andrew still didn't trust her.

Throughout the journey back to the surgery, they were both preoccupied with their own thoughts. Jess was sure Andrew would apologise. Instead, his silence made her heart plummet uncomfortably.

She hated the thought that he might go on believing she'd done such a thing, so she tried to work out another explanation for the note's disappearance. Lucy must be telling the truth, as the porter could too easily confirm or deny her story.

So, either the porter hadn't done as he claimed, or the

note had been removed. Who would want to do that? It
didn't make sense. It certainly hadn't been there when Jess
arrived, but there was no way Lucy was going to believe
her.

Andrew was another problem altogether. Even their rapport over lunch must have been a sham on his part. If she
hadn't heard the doubt in his voice with her own ears, she
wouldn't have believed it possible.

As he pulled into his designated parking space, he turned
to look at her with a bleak expression that made his eyes
resemble black marble.

'You didn't see a note, then?'

'Do I have to spell it out for you? What do you take me
for, Andrew Brent? A cheat and a liar? If that's what you
want to believe, I'll report back to the agency tomorrow
and they can find you someone else.'

She climbed from the passenger side of the car and,
slamming the door with a force she usually reserved for her
own box on wheels, she stalked away in the direction of
the surgery.

CHAPTER FIVE

ANDREW followed at a distance, calling after her, 'Jess, please.'

Ignoring him, she arrived at the waiting room door and rapidly searched the area in case the note had fallen out of sight. Finding no sign of it, she banged the door open, leaving no one in any doubt about her feelings.

Although startled by her entrance, Lucy was quickly on the offensive. 'So, with me out of the way, you persuaded Andrew to take you out to lunch, did you? Well, let me tell you, he and Sylvia—' She stopped abruptly as Andrew hurried in.

When he ignored them both, Lucy followed him into his consulting room. Jess took the opportunity to escape into the treatment room, where she started to noisily tidy the trolley whilst wondering what Lucy had been about to say about Sylvia.

Hearing raised voices, she smiled wryly to herself and switched on the kettle. Let them sort it out between them. She'd wasted enough time and effort.

She would remain where she was for the afternoon, but would certainly not return the next day. She hoped the agency wouldn't be able to find them a suitable replacement.

She made herself a cup of coffee and, before drinking it, checked no one was waiting to consult her or to register.

Her temper was still simmering when the door of the treatment room opened to admit Andrew. 'Jess. Lucy's gone for lunch, so could I have a word?'

She gazed at him stolidly but remained silent.

His gaze held hers unflinchingly, until the tension between them was almost unbearable.

Unable to endure it any longer, she turned to riffle abstractedly through the papers on her desk.

Sighing, Andrew used the hot water in the kettle to make himself a mug of coffee.

He pulled the hard-backed chair towards him, and straddled it the wrong way. With a deep sigh he began hesitantly to explain. 'Jess, I really didn't intend to suggest that you...' He paused, then continued with a sigh, 'Lucy was so dogmatic on the phone. I was so annoyed by her unnotified absence that when she came up with this tale I didn't know what to think. You must appreciate I've worked with her for a long time, and, although I was sure you were both speaking the truth, I was trying to puzzle out what could have happened. God! I guess I'm making an even greater fist of this explanation...'

Staring impassively, Jess made no attempt to help, though in her heart of hearts she was beginning to appreciate his dilemma. He *had* known Lucy for a couple of years, and had no reason to suspect she wasn't telling him the truth.

'Jess, I wasn't accusing you. I was merely trying to clarify things in my own mind. I—oh, what's the use? I just can't think straight...' He placed his arm on the hard back of the chair and rested his forehead down, hiding dark, bleary eyes.

Recalling his sleepless night, Jess recognised that it *could* excuse his earlier doubts. Her anger even began to resolve into a concern for him that tugged painfully at her heart.

'Forget it, Andrew. I guess I overreacted. Can't you take the remainder of the afternoon off?'

Lifting his head wearily, he yawned widely before saying, 'I think I will. There are no visits to do this end, and I can always be reached at home. I had intended going over to Roundings, to see that all was well there, but Lucy already did that when she took Gen, the girl with the broken leg, back to her room.

'Will Gen be all right getting around the site?'

'Her parents are taking her home this afternoon. The hospital thought it best.'

'The rest are OK, then?' Jess was surprised. She'd expected several visits might be necessary.

'Apparently so. Several of them have been back to the hospital this morning for follow-up checks, so we don't seem to be needed today. Rachel has seen Maria, and there's no problem there, and I can be easily contacted if I'm needed.'

'Have they found accommodation for those made roomless?'

'Luckily there weren't many occupied rooms in that wing of the block, so Rachel has managed to find empty ones in other parts of the building for those who had already moved in. The fire was mainly in the kitchen, where it started, and in the communal rooms. That's where most people were.'

Jess nodded, before asking tentatively, 'What about Ian, Andrew? Didn't you promise to call in and see him today?'

Andrew clapped a dismayed hand to his forehead. 'I clean forgot.' He paused unhappily. 'Thanks for reminding me. He's the last person I should let down.'

'I'll call on my way home and see if there's anything he needs,' Jess offered gently. 'You go and get some sleep.'

He nodded. 'I'd sure appreciate that. But I'm not going before I've convinced you that I'd like you to apply for the vacant position here. You're just the motherly type we need—oh, dear, that sounds dreadful.' He rested a repentant hand on her shoulder. 'I didn't mean to insult you—I just want to make it clear that you'd be the ideal person to join our team.' He paused, before adding almost jubilantly, 'You have to admit I wouldn't think that if I believed you'd tried to make trouble for Lucy, would I?'

The office telephone was clamouring for attention, so

Jess shrugged and went to answer it. While she did so, Andrew crossed to his room to sort out his desk.

As she replaced the receiver she saw the waiting room door open and, worried by the sight of a young student assisting an obviously distressed man through it, rushed to open the treatment room door.

'Mr Steel isn't very well,' the student told her unnecessarily as the older man staggered and clutched his chest, all the while sweating profusely.

He certainly isn't, Jess thought as she saw him grimace and stumble as the pain worsened.

'This way.' Jess tried to make the patient comfortable on her examination couch, all the while assessing his condition. Clearly in pain, with a weak and thready pulse, and the sweat was standing out on his cold skin. She was pretty sure it was a heart attack and asked the youngster if he was another student.

'No, he's my tutor—Tom Steel.'

She sped quietly across to Andrew. 'There's a member of staff in my room. I think—'

'Staff? I told you, we don't treat them—'

'Andrew,' she broke in impatiently, 'you will this one. It's an emergency. I think it's a heart attack.' She spun on her heels and raced back to check his condition. Andrew was close behind.

'Tom Steel,' she told him.

The frightened student with him murmured, 'He was talking about my assignment when he suddenly gasped and the colour seemed to drain from his face.'

Andrew nodded. 'Thanks. Could you wait outside now?' After a quick look at Tom, Andrew asked him, 'What's the pain like?'

'It's as if…' Tom gasped '…something squeezing, crushing my chest…'

Andrew nodded and told him, 'Don't try to talk any more. I'm going to check your pulse and blood pressure.' He did so, quickly and quietly, then said, 'Ring for an ambulance, Jess. Stress we need one with fully trained paramedics.' He turned back to his patient. 'Right, Tom, I'm going to do two things: I'm going to give you an injection to ease the pain, but first I want you to swallow an aspirin.'

When she was sure the ambulance was on its way, Jess joined the young student in the waiting room. 'I've told the ambulance to come to the door off car park five. Could you meet it there and show them where to come?'

Clearly relieved to escape from a scary situation, and yet do something useful, he nodded and raced off.

When Jess rejoined Andrew in the treatment room she could already hear the ambulance siren in the distance.

'Sounds like Tom's transport is on its way. Do they know where to find us?'

She smiled reassuringly. 'The student who brought Tom in has gone to meet them. There should be no problem.'

'In that case I'm not going to pull him about any more. They'll soon have him wired up to their monitor.'

The paramedics were super-efficient and quickly had Tom on a wheeled stretcher. Carrying his medical bag, Andrew followed them out, but once Tom was safely in the ambulance and wired up to their machines *en route* for the hospital, he returned.

'Thanks, Jess. You were so calm and yet left me with no option but to see him, and quickly. We definitely need you here permanently.'

He returned to his earlier attempt at persuasion. 'Having now watched you cope with more genuinely ill patients than I believe I've seen since the day I started here, I know there's no way we'll find anyone more suitable.'

'I'm sorry, Andrew, but I've no intention of making any decision at the moment.' She hesitated, then decided to say what was in her mind. 'Unless there's a distinct improvement in the atmosphere, I wouldn't want the job. Let's just see how things go, shall we?'

He sighed deeply. 'I suppose so.' He shrugged. 'I wish we could discover what *really* happened this morning.'

Jess shook her head resignedly. 'I don't think that's the only problem.'

'You don't?' He shook his head irritably. 'Oh! I *do* wish this fog would clear from my brain.'

Once again she felt concern for him tearing her apart. 'It won't until you get some sleep.' Before he could sense her tenderness towards him, which was rapidly becoming something more than maternal, she moved back into the office. 'Go home, for goodness' sake, before someone else arrives to delay you.'

He followed and rested a hand firmly on her shoulder. 'We'll continue this chat tomorrow. Let me know if there's any kind of a problem with Ian.'

Sliding out from beneath his hand, she set about sorting the afternoon's paperwork into neat piles for Lucy's attention. A move she was thankful to have made when Lucy rushed in breathlessly.

Jess handed the forms to Lucy and explained about her visit to Ian. 'So, if it's all right by you, I'll leave early and visit him on my way home.'

Lucy appeared more than happy to agree. 'I should go now, in case he *does* need things done.'

'Will you be all right on your own? I think Andrew's going home to grab some sleep.'

Lucy's answering look was withering. 'Are you suggesting I won't be able to cope?'

Telling herself that Lucy was no doubt kicking herself for packing Jess off early when Andrew was also leaving, she murmured in a conciliatory tone, 'Certainly not.'

At that moment the doctor emerged from his room with an armful of papers. Directing a brief nod towards both girls, he informed them, 'I've got the radio-pager—see you tomorrow.'

Prudently, Jess allowed a good half-hour to elapse before following. When she did consider it safe to leave, she pulled open the door to find a startlingly good-looking male about to push it from the other side.

His smart-suited appearance suggested he was not a student, so Jess enquired, 'Can I help you?'

Inquisitively Lucy bustled over and listened intently.

'Er, I think this is probably yours.' He handed over a folded piece of paper. 'I found it pinned to my office door upstairs.'

Jess was about to take it from him, when Lucy reached past and almost snatched it. 'I thought as much. It's my message from this morning. Now perhaps you'll both believe me.'

Jess swallowed with embarrassment, knowing there had been no question of anyone not believing *Lucy*. However, she saw no point in saying so and murmured, 'I'd better get over to Ian's.'

She set off along the corridor and as she did so, heard Lucy's voice plainly. 'Come on in and tell me where you found this.'

Jess stayed and chatted to Ian for most of the afternoon, so it was past her normal time when she arrived home.

'You must be shattered after your disturbed night,' Gwen greeted her.

'Not too bad,' Jess smiled. 'I've been so busy I haven't thought about it. And I had a cooked meal at lunchtime, so that helped.'

Gwen was immediately interested. 'I'm glad you're starting to look after yourself at last.'

Jess protested. 'I wasn't setting a precedent. I was treated to it.'

Gwen nodded approvingly. 'Well, whoever it was, I'm glad he's looking after you.'

'How did you know it was a ''he''?'

Gwen raised a noncommittal eyebrow. 'Just guessing.'

Although she didn't respond to Gwen's attempt to ferret out who she'd eaten with, Jess went about bathing and reading to Ruth aware that she had felt a contentment all day that she couldn't remember experiencing since Larry died.

It *really* didn't make sense—especially when she remembered Andrew's reaction to the missing note—but it perhaps explained why she had forgiven him so readily.

When Ruth eventually settled, Jess joined Gwen and Les for their meal. As they were finishing, the telephone's strident clamour broke the companionable silence.

Jess lifted the receiver to hear Andrew's voice at the other end. 'I seem to be making a habit of this. I—er—hope I'm not disturbing your meal, because I was hoping you might possibly be able to help me out?' He spoke hesitantly.

'Help you? How?'

'Can you leave your daughter again for a couple of hours?'

'I suppose so.' Jess was puzzled, so qualified her agreement by saying, 'If it's urgent.'

She heard a deep sigh at the other end of the line. 'Not exactly urgent, but I don't know what else I can do.'

'About what?' Jess prompted, unsettled by his not getting to the point.

'A student from one of the residential blocks on the main site has rung to say that one of our foreign students appears to have been, shall we say, assaulted. She's quite badly knocked about but refuses to talk to anyone. I know the girl—she came to the surgery frequently in her first year. She's excessively timid and keeps herself very much to herself. I think she trusts me, so I might be able to get through to her, but there's no way she'll allow another student in with us, and I'll be unable to examine her unless I have a female chaperon. I've tried to contact Lucy but she's out, so I just wondered…?'

'I'm sure Gwen won't mind, under the circumstances. Shall I meet you there?'

'No need for that.' He sounded relieved. 'I can easily pick you up. 17 Luccombe Gardens, isn't it?'

'That's right.'

He replaced his receiver, leaving Jess to wonder at him

locating her address so easily. She barely had time to clear away the dinner dishes and change her tracksuit for a softly draping red dress before the front doorbell rang.

Having already explained to Gwen and Les where she was going, Jess blew them both a kiss. 'Ruth shouldn't wake, and I'll be back as soon as I can.' She opened the door and hurried out to join Andrew.

He greeted her with a look of such intensity that when he took hold of her arm his touch scattered tiny flutters of pleasure the length and breadth of her body.

'This is very good of you, Jess.' He spoke softly and seductively, increasing her disturbing reaction to him. 'And I must say that colour does a lot more for you than your navy uniform.'

Scared she wouldn't be able to handle the situation if he continued to sprinkle his conversation with compliments, she countered archly, 'How could I refuse, when you asked so nicely?' Then, recalling the reason for their visit, she added more soberly, 'Seriously, I couldn't have done anything else. What that poor girl must be going through…'

Andrew nodded. 'I only hope it isn't as bad as it sounds. It's very difficult to gauge when these girls often leave a sheltered existence to come over here and study.'

As he spoke, they arrived at the student block. Without waiting for a reply, he lifted his bag, and when Jess joined him led the way to the main entrance.

Anna, the girl who had rung him, was waiting. 'She still refuses to open the door, Dr Brent. We don't know what else to do.'

'I think it best if you all disappear, Anna. I'll contact you before we leave, Your room number is?'

'241—but I'll wait down here so she won't be embarrassed. Kim's room is 242.'

Andrew nodded, and made his way up a couple of flights of stairs. His long stride took the steps two at a time, leaving Jess breathless as she tried to keep up with him. Arriving at Kim's door, he knocked gently. 'Hello, Kim.

It's Dr Brent. I've brought the nurse with me to see if we can do anything to help you. Anna tells us you've had an accident.'

Silence from within greeted his first few attempts, but suddenly Kim opened the door a crack and then, seeing he really was who he said, began to open it wider.

Jess gasped at the sight of her face. It was bruised and bleeding, with eye orbits so swollen it was impossible to say where one finished and the other began, let alone her nose.

'She not your nurse,' Kim complained, and pushed at the door, but Andrew's foot prevented it closing.

'Lucy isn't available. Jess has taken Joanne's place—she's our new nurse.'

Pulling her dressing gown even further round her body, Kim reluctantly allowed them to enter.

Andrew helped the young Malay girl to the one easy chair in the room, and motioned Jess to take the hard-backed seat beside the small desk. He seated himself on the edge of the bed and leaned over to examine the damaged face closely.

'What happened, Kim?' he asked gently.

Receiving no reply, he tried again. 'Kim, it will help me to assess the extent of the damage if I know how these injuries were caused. You know me well enough to believe that anything you say will go no further.'

The injured girl looked towards Jess.

Andrew shook his head, 'Jess's a professional.' He cast an admiring glance towards her. 'I trust her implicitly.'

The warmth that flooded to her cheeks made Jess thankful he had already returned his attention to Kim.

'Well?'

'I fell over.' The downcast eyes that accompanied her meek voice belied her statement.

'No, Kim,' Andrew admonished, gently but firmly. 'You'll have to do better than that. Where did this happen?'

With infinite patience, Andrew was eventually able to gently cajole the whole truth from the student.

'I—I'd been to the corner shop—you know, across the common.' She paused as if to gather some inner strength before continuing, 'It was getting dark, so I tried to hurry, but the plastic bag was heavy.'

As she haltingly told the story, tears cascaded down her face. Jess moved to crouch beside her and offer the support of a comforting arm.

'Someone took hold of me from behind.'

She went on to haltingly tell them how her unusual costume had foiled her attacker's frenzied attempts to rip it from her body. And how his resulting fury had caused him to repeatedly punch her face before stealing her purse and running off.

'I tried to creep back to my room without being seen, but I was shaking so much I couldn't unlock the door.' Kim was sobbing violently at the thought of what had happened to her.

'That must have been when Anna came out of her room and saw you?'

Kim nodded. 'I didn't want her to tell anyone. I was ashamed. Please, I don't want to go to the police or to go to hospital. I just don't want anyone to know.'

'We're not anyone,' Andrew told her gently. 'We're just here to help. Are you sure that's all that happened?'

As Kim nodded, Jess looked up towards Andrew and saw mirrored there her own relief. The physical scars were bad, but would heal. The emotional trauma would take much longer, but, if what Kim had told them was the whole truth, her purity had not been defiled. That would have been a trauma she would probably never have overcome.

As the girl's tears dried, Andrew gently and minutely examined her injuries with Jess's help. Straightening his back at last, he patted the patient's hand and seated himself back on the bed. 'I think you've been very lucky. As far as I can tell there's nothing permanent. We'll need to retest your eyesight when the swelling goes down a bit, and we can organise some head X-rays tomorrow at Outpatients, if you don't want to go into hospital tonight. But what you need most at the moment is a good night's sleep.' Andrew paused thoughtfully. 'But I don't want you left alone.'

He spoke again to Kim. 'Is there anyone who can be with you tonight?'

She shook her head emphatically. 'No one. I will be all right.'

Andrew shook his head. It was an impasse. He couldn't stay alone with the girl and Jess had a family to return to.

Recognising the problem, Jess whispered, 'Give me a few moments to ring home; I'll see what I can do.'

She was back almost immediately. 'Kim can have my bed. I'll keep an eye on her for the night.'

Andrew's look of gratitude was tinged with concern. 'Are you sure that won't cause problems with Ruth's grandparents?'

Jess smiled and shook her head. 'They're very understanding. They won't ask questions. They know she has injuries that need to be kept under observation overnight and that's all. I'll bring Kim back here in the morning.'

Wrapping a blanket around the slight girl, Andrew carried her down to his car while Jess locked the door.

As Andrew climbed into the driving seat Jess had a sudden thought. 'Kim? Were there any credit cards in your purse? Because if so we should notify someone.'

'Only cash.'

'And you were insured?'

The girl nodded. 'Through the union.'

'Fine. We can sort that out in the morning.' Jess smiled reassuringly.

When they arrived at Luccombe Gardens, Jess found Gwen and Les already asleep, and her own bed made up with clean bedding. They were able to settle Kim immediately, so, as they made their way downstairs again, Jess offered Andrew some refreshment.

'I've imposed on you far too much already, Jess. And I must call in at the hall and explain to Anna that Kim is in good hands. And then I need some sleep. I seem fated to be kept from my bed this week.' Taking both her hands in his, he looked deeply into her eyes. 'I have an awful lot to thank you for this evening.'

'I don't know about that,' Jess admitted ruefully. 'My gasp of horror at the sight of Kim's face nearly blew that visit. A good job your footwork was so neat.'

Andrew grinned wryly. 'A little trick learnt when I did some door-to-door selling as a student.'

'What did you hawk around?'

'Would you believe encyclopaedias?'

Jess shook her head. 'Not really.'

Andrew laughed. 'I'm not surprised. I wasn't very good at it. I only ever sold one.'

'I can't believe that, after witnessing your powers of persuasion this evening,' she teased.

'I couldn't have done any of it without your help.'

Jess laughed again. 'Wouldn't you rather continue this mutual admiration over a cup of coffee? I missed out on mine after dinner.'

'In that case I won't keep you from your dose of caffeine any longer, but I really must go. I'll see you tomorrow.'

Before he opened the front door he leant forward, and his lips met hers with a firm but gentle pressure that caused a small, but overheated volcano to erupt within her.

The fire that surged to every part of her body churned her insides to a long-forgotten turbulence that told her she would be foolish to allow him to repeat the kiss. She pushed him lightly away before he could notice the straining response of every fibre of her body.

He already had Sylvia in his life, and if they were to go on working together, allowing him to recognise how his body could affect her would be a recipe for disaster.

He met her rebuff with a deep and searching scrutiny of

her face before stepping closer to murmur, 'That was merely by way of a thank-you. The next one will be—'

She stopped him in mid-sentence. 'One too many. Goodnight, Andrew.' She opened the door and left him in no doubt as to what was required of him. Sighing, he gave her one last look of entreaty before striding agilely down the path and clambering into his car.

She watched him out of sight with a deep sense of relief that was more than a little tinged with regret, then crept silently upstairs to check on Kim. The girl was sleeping soundly and her steady pulse indicated all was well.

But, after securing the house downstairs and switching off the lights, when she slid into the spare bed in her daughter's room, Jess couldn't sleep.

She'd enjoyed her evening assisting Andrew. Difficult though their task had been, it had resulted in an improving rapport between them. Irrationally, she was no longer sure it was what she wanted, because the treacherous emotions his kiss had aroused within her had made her long for more.

But not to share him with Sylvia. If that was what his second kiss would have asked of her, she was relieved she had stopped him when she had, despite the thought of it making her skin tingle deliciously.

Ruth would be the one most hurt by such a liaison, and that was the last thing she was prepared to allow. No, she would be happy with an improvement in the working atmosphere, but nothing more. When the new appointment was made, she would finish her stint there without regrets.

That decision made, she slipped from her bed to check on Kim's condition, and, seeing again the battered face, knew she could have done nothing else but agree to help. She found it difficult to understand the mind of anyone who could so brutally attack a defenceless student.

The girl was still sleeping peacefully, so Jess made her way quietly downstairs and curled up in an armchair with a cup of hot chocolate. Her tortuous thoughts precluded any hope of sleep that night.

* * *

The rest of the family were up at the usual time, and Jess asked Gwen if she would mind taking Ruth to school for once.

'No problem. It'll be a treat for us both.'

When an inquisitive and wide-eyed Ruth left with her grandmother, and Les wandered out to his greenhouse, Jess took a cup of tea in to Kim and gently woke her. 'How do you feel this morning?'

The changing shades of her extensive bruising made her face look more painful than ever, but mentally Kim seemed brighter for her good night's rest.

'When you're ready we'll have some breakfast and then I'll take you to the hospital. We can hopefully be back at college before coffee break. Most people should have left the halls for lectures by that time. We can go straight to your room and Dr Brent will be over to have another look at you later.'

Kim nodded her gratitude. 'You are both so very kind. I feel so much better having told you about it.'

Jess nodded. 'It does help to talk over our troubles, doesn't it?'

Later, as they made their way out to the car, Jess wished there was some way *she* could act on her own advice. As it was, once she had seen Kim safely to her room, she would have to face Andrew. And she wasn't looking forward to it after her rebuff the previous night. Hopefully there would be no reference to it and she could pretend it had never happened.

Carrying a mug of coffee, Lucy was in the process of opening Andrew's door when Jess walked into the office.

'Huh. Better late than never, I suppose.' Lucy's terse comment made it clear Andrew hadn't explained why Jess would be late.

'There's your coffee,' Lucy slammed the mug down onto his desk, and, glancing towards Jess, suggested, 'Now you've both decided to put in an appearance, perhaps we could get the surgery underway. Several of the students have been waiting since nine.'

Jess took a deep breath and bit back her response as she wondered if Lucy was implying Andrew had only just beaten her to the surgery.

Dark eyes flashing furiously, he made no attempt to hide the fact that he wasn't exactly happy either.

'Come in, Jess.' He motioned her to the chair by his desk.

'Before you say anything more you'll regret, Lucy, bring Jess a coffee, too.' He snapped the order, adding perfunctorily, 'She looks in need of it.'

Lucy's mouth dropped open, and she was about to argue when Andrew lifted his head and through narrowed eyes gave her a look so dark that it sent her scurrying away to do his bidding without a word.

His expression changed completely as, silently, he turned to Jess, his searching eyes showing a concern she hadn't bargained for.

As she waited for him to speak her coffee was banged down, as Andrew's had been, and Jess couldn't help an irrepressible grin springing to her lips.

'We'll start seeing the patients in a moment, Lucy. In the meantime, close the door behind you,' Andrew ordered. 'I need to talk to Jess.'

Lucy's jaw could not have dropped any further without dislocating. And despite her resolve to limit their discussions to work topics, the thought of Lucy's incredulity kept the smile hovering around Jess's lips as she turned to face him.

'How's Kim?' he asked quietly.

She could answer that—it concerned a patient. 'Much better. I took her to hospital, then straight to the hall of residence to prevent any questions being asked.'

'Good. Good. I'll go and see her later. Did she sleep well?'

'Surprisingly well.'

'Which is more than you did,' he murmured softly, awareness plain on his face.

'That's not surprising, is it?' Jess retorted spiritedly, determined not to allow his concern to invade her emotions again. 'The reason I took her home was to keep a regular check on her.'

'Mmm. I want to thank you for doing that for me. I—'

Before he could start to discuss the other events of the evening, Jess rose from her chair. 'I did it for Kim, not you.' Ignoring his gasp of surprise, she said, 'I must get out to help Lucy now, or the surgery will go on for ever.'

CHAPTER SIX

CLOSING Andrew's door behind her, Jess met Lucy's hostile glare with equanimity. 'Andrew couldn't contact you last night so he called me out. I spent the night looking after a student who had been mugged. I have no idea why Andrew was late this morning. Now can we get on with the morning's work?'

Lucy stared open-mouthed at Jess before asking, 'Who—?'

'I think the questions can wait until later, don't you?' The tone of her interruption was calmly indifferent and remained so as she went on to enquire, 'Would you like me to start seeing those waiting for one of us?'

Taken aback by Jess's confident control of the situation, Lucy stammered out her reply, 'Y-yes—yes. You do that. I'll carry on out here.'

And hopefully that's made my position clear to both of them, Jess told herself wryly as she called in the first student waiting to be seen. Only if she was allowed to work without interference would she continue to help them out until the new appointment was made.

When the surgery finished, however, and a listless Andrew begged another cup of coffee to keep him going, she found herself sympathising in a way she hadn't intended. 'I suppose you didn't get a chance to catch up on your sleep last night?'

'Not really. Then I overslept, by which time the traffic was so horrific I was later than ever arriving. Lucy was far from overjoyed to find neither of us here on time.'

Jess made coffee for them all. As Andrew drained his mug, he looked up and asked, 'When I've finished this can we go over and visit Kim? I think this is one case where continuity of care is essential.'

Jess looked towards Lucy, expecting her to protest, but she merely nodded her agreement. 'I'll go to lunch when you get back.'

Thankful that Andrew must have explained about the previous night's visit, Jess indicated she was ready and reached for her coat.

'Come on, Jess. Don't stand there all day gossiping,' Andrew teased half-heartedly as he made his way towards the door carrying his briefcase.

She hurried to join him and they walked briskly over to the halls. Jess broke the tense silence between them by asking, 'Have you heard anything about that tutor—you know, the one with the heart attack?'

'Tom. Tom Steel. Yep, I rang up earlier. He's stabilised well.'

'That's great news,' Jess responded as they arrived at Kim's door.

Obviously feeling much better for her good night's sleep, the young student appeared pleased to see them both.

Andrew carefully examined the damage to her face again.

'You've been very lucky. I don't think there should be any permanent scarring and the X-rays were clear. How are you feeling in yourself?'

'A lot better, thank you, Dr Brent. And thank you, too, Nurse.'

Andrew smiled. 'Have you done anything about the in-surance?'

Kim shook her head. 'I prefer not to, thank you. It was not a lot of money and I don't want people to know.'

Andrew nodded. 'OK. I understand. One of us will pop in again later this afternoon, and we'll take another look at you tomorrow. In the meantime, you know where we are if you need us.'

As he closed the door behind him, he murmured, 'That

lass has a lot to thank you for. You caring for her last night has lessened the trauma greatly. If she'd been left here on her own I hate to think what state she might be in today. As it is, she's coping.'

Despite her earlier resolve, the sensuous look that accompanied his words snatched Jess's breath away. Thankful that he didn't appear to be expecting a reply, she accompanied him back to the health centre with her thoughts working overtime.

When Lucy had gone to lunch she produced her box of sandwiches and, after offering one to Andrew, bit reflectively into her own.

'Have you thought any more about the job here?'

She shook her head. 'As I said, I think I'm better off with the agency. They pay well, too.'

'I hear what you are saying, but if you're on our staff, at least you'll have regular work. There must be times when the agency have nothing to offer. If that happened often, how would you exist?'

Jess smiled wryly. 'It's a very rare occurrence. The shortage of trained nurses in the area has been so acute that the agency have usually found something.'

'Always the kind of work you want?'

'Well, no. Not exactly. And I have done the odd shift in a nursing home. But it keeps me in touch with a wide range of skills.'

'Don't forget if you work for us you'll get holiday pay, and benefit, should you be ill.'

'Don't you know? These days the agencies pay all that, if you work for them on a regular basis, and they also pay my National Insurance contributions.'

Andrew's face registered surprise. 'Agencies have certainly changed since my day, then.'

'Some of them have, and I work for one of the best.'

'So,' Andrew muttered, 'our offer can't compete, then?'

'Not really,' Jess agreed.

'But what about the hours you have to work? When I

met Ruth in the supermarket she was obviously enjoying having you home each evening.'

Jess grimaced. 'I know. But if I specify these hours I don't earn the same money—and there aren't many suitable places.'

'So you haven't completely ruled us out?'

Jess shrugged non-committally. 'It would be nice to have the regular money and always be home for Ruth, but...' She hesitated.

'In that case I might be able to extract a small increase in salary for the right qualifications, and I can vouch for yours. And, should Ruth be ill, we can always come to some arrangement so that you can be home with her. At least apply before the closing date, Jess, and I'll see what can be done.'

She was torn. She'd proved he could rely on her work, so now he wanted her to stay. A regular salary and being home each evening *was* tempting, but she wasn't sure she could continue to work closely with him without revealing her confused feelings about him—because that was what they were. Totally confused. Especially when, as today, he was being so considerate he displayed a charisma she couldn't ignore.

She sighed. 'All right. I will apply. But at the moment I don't guarantee I'll accept the post, even if I'm offered it. A lot depends on how we all work together over the next couple of weeks.'

'It should only get better. Lucy is very sorry to have accused you of destroying her note. Come to that, why didn't you tell me last night that it had turned up?'

'I didn't consider it important.'

He raised an eyebrow sceptically, then laughed. 'I'll believe you. Thousands wouldn't—especially if they'd witnessed your fury at my accusation.'

'What did you expect?' she retorted huffily.

'Certainly not what I got, but it made me have second

thoughts about making your position here permanent.' He laughed.

'Because of my temper?'

'Certainly not. I was worried that you were going to walk out on us. So, I'll get the office to send up an application form and job description this afternoon. As you are going home the moment Lucy reappears, you can pick it up tomorrow and complete it over the weekend.'

'Are you sure I won't be needed this afternoon. I—'

'You'll do as you're told. Right? We'll start the way we mean to go on.'

He was still chuckling when Lucy came back in.

'What's the joke?'

As Jess hesitated uncertainly, Andrew explained, 'Jess was worried about leaving us to cope this afternoon. I just told her she is not indispensable.'

Lucy frowned, apparently puzzled as to why this should cause hilarity, but surprisingly accepted the explanation without comment.

As she walked out to her car, Jess had to admit she appreciated his thoughtfulness. It was lovely to get home for a leisurely cup of tea before picking Ruth up from school.

Gwen and Les decided to make the most of their unexpected free afternoon and drive over to the next town to visit friends.

Ruth was bathed and climbing into bed that evening when the doorbell rang. 'You stay there,' Jess ordered.

She ran lightly down the stairs and was surprised to find Andrew on the doorstep.

'Hi. When the job application form arrived this afternoon, I discovered the closing date is tomorrow. So I came round, as I think you might need information you won't necessarily have with you.' Clearly anxious to justify his presence, he added, 'You know what I mean, don't you? Registration numbers, dates and the like.'

Aware that he was expecting to be invited in, Jess explained, 'I'm just getting Ruth into bed, so if you'll ex-cuse—'

'That was partly why I came round at this time,' he ex-plained diffidently. 'I'd like to see her again. Just for a few minutes.'

His request took Jess by surprise, and she stumbled over her reply. 'I—I d-don't see why not. You'd better come in.' She opened the door wider to admit him, and grinned as she recognised he already had one foot in the door.

'Selling something, Dr Brent?' she teased.

'Only myself.'

He didn't enlarge on his statement, but his seductive tone rocked her resolve of the previous evening, leaving her breathless and expectant.

Starting up the stairs, she said, 'I'll bring Ruth down for a moment—'

Andrew broke in quickly. 'Don't disturb her routine. I'll come up.' He followed Jess into the child's bedroom.

'Hello? What are you doing here?' Ruth asked, with the bluntness of childhood.

'I had to call by and thought it would be nice to see you again.'

'You're nice, 'cos you let my mummy off early so she could meet me after school today.'

He grinned. 'She did that? When I'd sent her home for a rest? You've got a kind mummy, then, haven't you?'

Ruth nodded. 'I love her. Do you?'

'Ruth!' Jess exclaimed in horror as the colour flamed in her cheeks.

The little girl pouted, unsure what she had done wrong.

He patted her hand consolingly. 'I like having her work with me very much. I hope she'll be able to stay for a long time.'

Ruth had clearly forgotten Jess's warning not to pester him. She demanded he read her a story. When it was fin-ished, he kissed her goodnight, saying quietly to Jess, 'I'll wait downstairs. I don't want to get her so excited she won't sleep.'

'I won't be long. I'll get some coffee when I come down.' Her mind hardly aware of the words, Jess read a couple more stories before tucking up her daughter and leaving her to sleep. She ran down the stairs to find Andrew examining the various photographs on the sideboard.

He turned to Jess with a look of utter horror on his face.

Jess frowned. 'Something wrong?'

He picked up a photograph of Larry and thrust it towards her. 'Is this Ruth's father?'

'Ye—es?' She couldn't imagine why he was so angry.

'Larry Halton was Ruth's father?' he asked again, disbelief dripping from every word.

'Yes, but I don't see what it has to do with you.'

Andrew sat down heavily. 'You didn't visit him when he was dying.' He made the statement in a flat voice. 'Whatever he'd done in the past, you might have made a difference to the outcome—even if you'd come only as the mother of his child.

'As it was, though we fought and fought to save him, and thought we were winning, he died. He appeared to have nothing to live for. News of you and his child could have made all the difference.'

Her face white with fury and disbelief, Jess drew a deep breath and said through tight lips, 'It's nothing to do with you. I'd like you to leave now, please.'

'Nothing to do with me? I was the doctor who looked after him. I had to look twice at the photograph, but when I saw it was signed "Larry" I knew I was right. He's one of those patients that stick in your memory because you feel you've failed them.'

'You don't know what you're talking about,' she told him heatedly.

'He was so easy to get on with. His mother gave us one of your letters she'd found in his belongings, so we could try and contact you. But it was too late by that time.' He hesitated, then added, 'You didn't want him to go to Bangladesh, did you? Was that why you didn't visit?'

'I don't want to discuss this. Please leave now.'

He shook his head in disbelief. 'I've been completely taken in by you. Only someone with a heart carved from marble could have treated Larry that way. And I thought you were such a caring person.' He turned on his heel and left the house, slamming the door behind him.

Jess closed her eyes and took a deep breath to steady herself. To avoid thinking how differently the evening might have gone if it hadn't been for fate decreeing otherwise, she dished up the food Gwen had prepared earlier. But she had no appetite, and pushed it round and round the plate.

As they'd shared Ruth's bedtime, she had sensed a heightening awareness between them that, despite her reservations, had excited her. Indeed, watching him with Ruth, she had even questioned whether she was right to say there was no room for him in their lives.

He had cruelly destroyed all that by jumping to a totally erroneous conclusion. One which was even more distressing when only that day he'd indicated he was so impressed with her work that he wanted her to fill the health centre vacancy permanently.

It was something he must now regret, but he could at least have given her a chance to explain. Unless—unless he'd sensed her feelings towards him changing and Larry's photograph had offered him the escape he was looking for. That thought flooded her face with heat. Perhaps he *had* come to the house that evening for nothing more than to bring her the form.

But, if so, why had he been so keen to see Ruth again? It was almost as if he was checking up on her—hadn't he questioned Jess about her childcare arrangements since her first day at the health centre?

Too upset to work it out, she tipped the untasted food into the wastebin. She should have explained the situation to him the first time he had asked, but recalling the events surrounding Larry's death still affected her deeply and the last thing she had wanted to do was make a fool of herself.

She took herself off to bed before Gwen and Les returned. Having locked her door behind her, she wept bitterly as thoughts of Larry and Andrew churned around in her mind. It just didn't seem fair that of all the doctors there must be in the country, Andrew had to be the one who'd looked after him.

And yet, the more she thought about the number of medics she had worked with since joining the agency, it would probably be more peculiar if one of them hadn't been on the team. Especially as the hospital Larry had been in was just along the M4 corridor from Bradstoke. The medical world was so comparatively small that it was a frequent occurrence to meet up with former colleagues in new jobs.

Eventually exhausted, she slept, but it was a restless and unhappy sleep.

She climbed from her bed at the usual time, and went through the motions of getting Ruth ready for school, undecided whether to return to the health centre that morning.

'Will the nice doctor come and read me another story tonight?' Ruth demanded as Jess struggled to persuade her to eat her breakfast.

'I doubt it,' Jess snapped, having seen interest flaring in Gwen's eyes.

'Why not? He's nice.'

'Because he's busy.'

'When won't he be?'

'I don't know,' Jess answered impatiently, her voice rising angrily as she added, for both Ruth and Gwen's benefit, 'He only called by to drop in a piece of paper.'

Ruth became subdued and stopped nibbling at her piece of toast.

'Hurry up and finish that, or you'll be late for school.'

Her eyes downcast, Ruth reluctantly did as she was told, then went in search of her coat.

Jess sensed Gwen's disapproval at her losing her temper for no apparent reason and murmured, 'I'm afraid I didn't sleep very well.'

'Would you like me to take Ruth to school?'

Jess shook her head. 'It'll give me a chance to make amends.'

By the time Ruth left her at the school gates they were good friends again, and the little girl waved happily as she ran across to the building.

Still not sure what to do as she walked away, Jess suddenly recalled Lucy's accusation of unreliability, and knew if she wasn't to reinforce that opinion for all agency nurses in the future she could do nothing else but turn up for work for one more day.

Running his fingers abstractedly through his hair, Andrew seated himself behind his desk with a groan.

Thoughts of Jess had kept him awake most of the night, and as he'd heard the nearby church clock strike every hour, he'd repeatedly berated himself for walking out without giving her a chance to explain.

At first he had been relieved to discover the truth about her before revealing what he'd been there for, but as the night had progressed he'd become increasingly sure that a caring person like Jess must have had a good reason for not visiting Larry.

He couldn't believe he had acted so stupidly, and could only put it down to his own sense of failure at not being able to save someone so important to Ruth and Jess.

Even before he'd discovered who her father was, Ruth had charmed her way into his heart. So much so that he had imagined himself getting to know her much better, and perhaps finding ways to make life easier for both her and her mother.

Even if that was now out of the question, there was no reason why the child should suffer. Quite the reverse. He'd like to do something for Larry's child. If working regularly at the college health centre meant Jess would be home each evening to put Ruth to bed, it would surely benefit the child. And there was no doubt Jess would be an asset.

Wearily, he opened his door to call through the first patient, and came face to face with Jess walking through from the waiting room. His heart contracted uncomfortably at the sight of the panda-sized shadows surrounding her eyes and he recognised at that moment that his attraction to her was stronger than ever.

'Hello, Jess. Is everything all right?'

'Fine.' her answer was clipped, and, ignoring him, she walked straight through the office to the treatment room.

Anguished by her snub, he wanted to follow her and try to explain. Instead he had to settle to his first consultation of the morning, aware that it was neither the time nor the place to bare his soul, and that even if it had been, she wouldn't listen.

Lucy followed her into the treatment room. 'Are you all right, Jess?'

That was a turn-up for the books—Lucy concerned about how she felt! Jess struggled to control her amusement. 'Yes. Why shouldn't I be?' Without giving Lucy a chance to reply, she continued, 'Shall I start seeing the patients in here now?'

'If that's what you'd like to do.' Lucy searched Jess's face relentlessly as she spoke.

'I'd prefer that, yes. Who's first?'

'A couple of girls wanting repeat prescriptions for the pill. Both just need routine checks.'

Jess nodded and called the name on the first set of notes Lucy handed to her.

Throughout a busy morning, she carried out her consultations almost mechanically. Thank goodness it was Friday; she had only agreed to remain for a second week and Lucy couldn't accuse her of dereliction of duty if she left that evening.

Towards lunchtime she could work no longer without a mug of coffee to revive her. She popped her head round the door, 'Coffee, Lucy?'

The other girl nodded gratefully. 'I could murder one.'

When the kettle boiled, she joined Jess in the treatment room for a quick break.

'How's it going?'

'All right. I'm getting through the list quite quickly.'

'You look tired. Do you find it hard to work here and then go home to your daughter?'

Jess shook her head. 'I'm very lucky, really. Her grandparents do most of the work. I just get the pleasure.'

Lucy nodded. 'Andrew told me yesterday you were thinking of applying for Joanne's job.'

'Not any more.' Jess intended Lucy should be in no doubt.

'I wish you would.'

Jess looked at Lucy in amazement. 'I thought I'd be the last person you'd want.'

Lucy shook her head. 'No. I could work with you.' She shrugged ashamedly. 'I know I didn't exactly welcome you at first.' She hesitated before admitting, 'After what the agency told him about you, Andrew was so sure you were ideal that I saw you as a threat. He's always criticising my lack of counselling skills.'

Jess smiled and rested a hand on Lucy's arm to reassure her. 'Then it's up to him to arrange training. None of us can be automatically good at everything. I'm not so hot on administration, but you do a marvellous job on the paperwork. Don't put yourself down, Lucy.'

She laughed. 'There you go again. You don't seem to have to make any effort to make me feel better, and it's the same with the students. Perhaps if we work together long enough some of your expertise will rub off on me.'

Jess sighed deeply. 'I don't think I'll be here after today.'

Lucy looked aghast. 'Why ever not? We need someone

until we get a replacement for Joanne, and you fit the bill perfectly.'

'It's nice of you to say so, but I'm sure the agency will find you someone just as good.'

'But what about you? Wouldn't you prefer to work the more regular hours?' She continued hesitantly, 'Don't you like the work?'

Jess smiled. 'It's been a pleasant change, but I just don't think it'll be a good idea to stay here any longer.'

Andrew came in at that moment. 'This is where everybody is. And where's my coffee?'

Jess turned back to the notes of her waiting patients and ignored him, while Lucy rushed to reboil the kettle.

Seemingly oblivious to the hostility between her colleagues, Lucy was determined to have her say. 'Jess says she won't be back next week, Andrew. You must persuade her. You said yourself we wouldn't find anyone else so perfect for the job.'

Andrew shrugged before appraising the view of Jess's back hopelessly. 'We'll chat about it at lunchtime—there's work to be done at the moment.' He returned to his own room, carrying his coffee with him.

Lucy watched him with bewilderment. 'What's eating him this morning, I wonder?'

Jess murmured non-committally and called in the next patient, a hockey player who had sustained a painful abrasion on the shin in a match a couple of days before. Jess thought it might be infected, but once she had cleaned it thoroughly, it looked much better. 'When was your last tetanus booster?' she asked the girl.

The student looked sheepish. 'A long time ago! Dr Brent said I needed one last time I was here, and I promised to come back and see the nurse, but I don't like injections and chickened out.'

'In that case, you're not leaving until I've given you a booster. Do you know what tetanus is?'

The girl nodded. 'I know it can paralyse muscles, including those we breathe with, but I didn't think I was likely to get it. I don't have anything to do with animals.'

Drawing up the booster dose of tetanus vaccine into the syringe, Jess shook her head despairingly. 'It doesn't need to be animals. Sportsmen and women are some of the people most at risk. The spores live in the soil, so every time your skin is broken on the hockey field, you could be infected.'

'Oh. I see.' She pulled her sleeve up to allow Jess to inject the vaccine. As Jess withdrew the needle, she said, 'Gosh, I didn't feel that at all.'

'Good. I'm going to give you a card now, so that you'll know when the next one is due. And remember, no excuses next time. And if you're worried about that leg, pop back again.'

'Thanks, Nurse.'

Jess completed the morning with a run of routine consultations, and her last patient was Fran, for the smear they had booked on Jess's first day there.

The moment Jess was free, Lucy asked anxiously. 'Do you mind if I go to lunch? I've arranged to meet someone.'

'That's fine. Has Andrew finished?'

'His last patient is in now.'

'Don't rush back—I've brought my usual sandwich.'

Lucy nodded gratefully and departed in a frantic rush, leaving Jess to wonder who it was that Lucy didn't want to keep waiting.

By the time Jess came in with his lunchtime coffee, Andrew was convinced that he was as mistaken about her behaviour towards Larry as he had been about her work.

As she handed him a mug, he saw a sadness in her eyes that, like her demeanour throughout the morning, told him clearly that she'd been hurt, deeply hurt in the past, and was hurting again.

He'd made things worse, much worse. He was the one

in the wrong. Twice now he'd judged her, without hearing the evidence.

How could he have doubted even for a moment someone who had behaved so compassionately to Kim and to the hysterical girls at the fire the night before that?

Recalling his determination to persuade her to fill the vacant post, he asked quietly, 'Have you completed the application form?'

'You ask me that after last night? I don't believe this, Andrew Brent. You are something else altogether.'

He recoiled uncomfortably at the scathing tone of her voice. 'I'm sorry. More than sorry, in fact. I should at least have given you a chance to explain—'

'You're sorry, are you? Well, so am I. Sorry I ever came here. Sorry I ever met you. And sorrier still that I ever allowed myself to consider becoming Joanne's replacement.'

He flinched at her bitterness, and, turning, carried his coffee out into the office and placed it on the desk, before following her into the treatment room.

He attempted to take hold of one of her hands, wanting somehow to make her listen. Jess was too quick for him. As his hand reached towards her she moved to the other side of the room and pretended to study the notes of her last patient.

'Jess, can't we talk?'

She glared at him with narrowed eyes. 'About work?'

'No, about last night.'

'I have nothing more to say on that subject.'

'I have. I—'

'I think you said all that was needed last night. Now, I'd be grateful if you'd leave me in peace to complete this paperwork.'

He didn't move immediately, but when she didn't look up, he sighed and made his way back to his own consulting room.

When she eventually emerged into the office, he watched

her silently for several minutes before broaching the subject again. 'Jess, I can imagine how you feel—'

'You can?' She was clearly determined not to allow him to explain. 'Fine. So, now we both know, I'd appreciate it if we could drop the subject.' She proffered her sandwich box towards him, and without thinking he took one.

They both ate in silence. Andrew knew they had reached an impasse that was impossible to resolve under the present circumstances, and he spent the remainder of his lunch-hour trying to think of a different approach to the problem.

Having finished but not enjoyed her sandwich, Jess returned to the treatment room. There was no way she wanted to talk to him or allow him to question her about Larry.

It was with relief that she heard a bubbly Lucy return to the office and come immediately in search of her.

'Did you have a good lunch?' Jess sensed Lucy wanted her to ask.

'Fantastic. I met Grant.' Her eyes were shining. 'You remember—the new lecturer who brought my note down the other day. We went out to The Feathers—oh, Jess, he's really cool.'

Amused that Lucy was now treating her as a confidante, Jess said she was pleased to hear it. 'Is this the first time you've met up with him?'

'No, we went for a drink last night. He's fantastic— good-looking, kind and thoughtful—everything I could want in a man.'

'And unmarried?' Jess couldn't help asking.

Lucy gave her a very straight look. 'Of course—what do you take me for?'

Jess repeated the old joke with a grin. 'It's not you, it's those lecturers. I was told long ago that "lecher-er" was a very good description of many of them.'

'I know. But Grant definitely isn't married. I asked him.'

'Go for it, then. I hope everything works out for you.'

It was Lucy's turn to grin. 'It will, as long as you agree to stay on here.'

Jess hesitated. 'Lucy, I—I—'

'You said yourself that we complement one another. You like the practical work and the counselling. I'm happier running the place.'

'I know, but—'

'And Andrew wants you to stay.'

'I don't think so, Lucy. I think you'll find he's changed his mind.'

There was no way she wanted to discuss her problems with Lucy, but she felt sure it wasn't going to be easy to convince her without doing so. 'Lucy, I—'

She was wrong. Lucy was too full of her own plans to care. 'He hasn't,' she broke in excitedly. 'We were talking while he finished his coffee, and he said then he was going to persuade you to apply.'

Jess shook her head doubtfully. 'I really think I'm better remaining with the agency. For my daughter's sake. I'm sorry, Lucy, but I promise I'll keep in touch.'

To change the subject, she asked, 'What time are you and Andrew leaving for the other surgery?' It couldn't be soon enough for Jess.

Lucy looked surprised. 'We're not.' She frowned. 'Didn't Andrew say? *You're* going with him.'

Jess wasn't quick enough to think up an excuse. 'I thought you preferred to do that?'

'No. Unfortunately I need to catch up on all this.' Lucy gestured towards the untidy pile of registration forms that Jess had to admit was threatening to submerge the desk.

'When was that decided?'

'Oh, before I went to lunch. That's all right, isn't it? You are working this afternoon, aren't you?'

Jess sighed. 'I'm afraid so.'

'It must be a long day for you.' Lucy clearly thought she meant she would rather not be working at all, and Jess didn't attempt to correct her assumption.

CHAPTER SEVEN

WHEN Andrew indicated it was time to leave, Jess got ready without a word.

As they made their way to the car park, a young girl came running towards them and Jess saw it was Andrea, who had been so homesick on her first day. She flung her arms round Jess. 'You were right. I can't thank you enough for making me see sense. I've lots of friends now.'

'I'm pleased to hear it.' Jess smiled, whilst freeing herself from the girl's grasp. 'I'm sure you'll have a great time from now on.'

As Andrew unlocked the car and helped her into the passenger seat, Jess experienced a quiet satisfaction at his having witnessed another example of her suitability for the post. She hoped he'd live to regret his behaviour the night before.

His normal poise clearly ruffled, he climbed behind the steering wheel and, firing the engine, said, 'Can't we return our relationship to the footing it was on before last evening?'

'What relationship?' she snapped. 'We worked together, that's all. And even then you didn't expect much of me.'

'Surely we were friends as well?'

'Acquaintances,' she corrected starchily, unwilling to meet him even halfway.

'Jess, can't we forget last night ever happened? I know I was out of order and I would like to explain—'

'There's nothing to explain, Andrew. Let's just drop the subject.'

He sighed deeply and, although they were nearly at the

Roundings site, he swung the car off the road into a small clearing and parked beneath an enormous chestnut tree.

'What—?' Angrily, Jess turned to him.

'I just want to talk to you somewhere you can't run away and refuse to listen, and also somewhere free from interruptions, well-meaning or otherwise.'

Conscious he was referring to Lucy, she told him, 'I've nothing to say to you, Andrew. What happened in my past has nothing to do with you, and I have no intention—'

'Just listen a minute, Jess.' A restrained tremor in his voice left Jess in no doubt he was having difficulty in remaining calm. 'I'm not demanding explanations. All I'm asking at the moment is that you'll apply for the job. For Lucy's sake and the sake of our patients—'

Jess could contain herself no longer. She laughed derisively. 'You're being a bit over-dramatic, aren't you? No one is that indispensable.'

Andrew laid a reassuring hand on her arm. 'Jess,' he said persuasively, 'you don't know what a relief it's been knowing you were seeing the patients. Joanne was a lovely girl, but she had no general practice experience. Consequently she referred nearly everything on to me, or, if not, the students came back to me themselves, saying they weren't satisfied.'

When she didn't reply, he sighed deeply.

'You're the ideal candidate for the post. Lucy knows what she's doing, and runs the place extremely efficiently, but even she finds difficulty in dealing with some of the students. You could teach her a lot. Your maturity gives you insight. And that isn't an insult about your age, either,' he placated with a half-hearted attempt at humour.

She responded with a sideways glance, but didn't speak.

He hesitated before adding despairingly, 'My workload some weeks has been unbelievable. Despite my disturbed nights, this has been the easiest week for me in a very long time. I really do want you to stay.'

Jess's heart contracted at the thought of him working so

hard—proving against all the odds that she still cared far too much about him. Resolutely she pushed the notion from her mind, and, lifting her chin determinedly, said, 'I can't see us ever working together harmoniously.'

It hurt like hell to rebuff him in this way, but it was for the best.

'I know, after the way I behaved, it's not an easy decision, but this job is where you belong and I'm asking you to reconsider. I'm sure it'll be much better for Ruth if you can get home each evening. And it'll be even more important as she gets older.'

Recognising the truth of what he was saying, Jess stared silently through the windscreen, her thoughts tumbling haphazardly. Why did he have to be so considerate again? If he'd just wanted her to stay for selfish reasons, she'd have found no difficulty in refusing, but he had to go and prove that he wasn't only thinking of himself.

'I think the three of us could make a great team.' He broke in persuasively on her thoughts. 'What do you say? Shall we give it a try?'

Jess remained silent.

'I promise never to mention the past again.'

She shrugged. 'It's not exactly that, Andrew. You've disturbed memories that I thought I'd got under control long ago, and knowing you looked after Larry is going to make it difficult to keep them in the past, where they belong.'

'Jess—' He began to protest, but she wasn't to be deterred.

'In other words, I'm not sure I can stand the strain—the strain of wondering what you're thinking now, whether my past will prevent you ever trusting me completely, because if not, I can see you doubting everything I do. You're quick enough to do that already.'

Andrew appeared pained by her accusation. He moved his hand gently up and down her arm. 'Jess, I have no worries at all where your work is concerned.'

Conscious he was pointedly referring only to her work,

while his stroking movement was driving the nerve-endings of her skin into a frenzy, she abruptly pulled her arm free.

'It won't work, Andrew. I think it would be much better if you ask the agency for a replacement from Monday and we never see one another again.'

'Can't we just give it a try? I know I'm rushing you, but the closing date for Joanne's post is today.' He gestured helplessly. 'I don't want you to miss it and then regret it, and you can always refuse the job at interview if in the meantime you find it really isn't working.' He turned to her with a sudden worried frown. 'You haven't told the agency you're finishing here today, have you?'

'No. But I intended to. It's only because I've been so busy I didn't find a moment to do so.'

That piece of news obviously encouraged him. 'Right. That's agreed, is it? I suppose as it's nearly two we'd better move.'

Jess was not at all sure she'd agreed to anything, but at least neither had she committed herself irrevocably. She could escape at any time, and in the meantime she would make the most of the easy hours and spend as much time with Ruth as possible. Starting with the coming weekend.

Andrew pulled up in front of the Roundings site. 'Let's hope it won't be too busy—I can't say I feel much enthusiasm for another surgery today.'

Conversely hoping they would be fully occupied for every moment of the two hours, Jess was uncommunicative as she followed him into the building. She was relieved to see a large group of students waiting to register. The last thing she wanted at that moment was to be alone with him, as they had been her first day there. The memory of that visit was far too vivid without a repetition.

One student she was especially pleased to see was Zoe, who had burnt her hand on the night of the fire when she'd gone back into the burning building to search for her engagement ring. 'I just came to say thank you to you both. My hand is much better. I had it dressed at the hospital again this morning, and they don't want to see me again, but they said I should give you this letter.'

Jess scanned its contents quickly and nodded. 'They are very pleased with how it's healing, aren't they? We'll be here on Monday if you want us to redress it.'

The girl smiled. 'I'll remember that.'

Once all the registrations were complete, Andrew carried out health checks on those who could wait, so they were kept busy way beyond the normal surgery finishing time.

The moment Jess had locked up, they went to visit Ian. 'I managed to get him an emergency appointment this morning,' Andrew told her. 'So I thought we'd see how he got on.'

'Thanks for getting things moving, Dr Brent,' Ian greeted them. 'They're booking me in for lots of investigations but they think I'll probably have to start dialysis soon. Then I should have much more energy. And I'm already provisionally on the list for a donor organ. They don't waste any time, do they?'

Andrew grinned. 'I'm pleased to hear it. Let's hope things keep moving so quickly. The sooner they confirm the cause, and get on with any treatment necessary, the better. In the meantime, let us know if you have any problems.'

'I sure will. The hospital doctor said he would be writing to you.'

He nodded. 'They always keep us informed, but the letters do take their time to reach me, so keep us up-to-date with developments, there's a good chap.'

Ian nodded. 'What about lectures?'

Andrew was thoughtful for a moment. 'We don't want you overdoing it, but I see no reason for you not to go when you feel up to it. We'll leave each day to your common sense, shall we? In the meantime, with your permission, I'll have another chat with your tutors, so that they'll understand when you aren't able to get in.'

'That'd be great, thanks. They shouldn't be surprised. I

sent a note to the department saying I had this appointment with the kidney specialist.'

Andrew nodded his approval and they took their leave from a much happier final-year student.

It was late by the time they arrived back at the main site, but Andrew pressurised her again. 'You'll come in now and complete the application form, won't you?'

Jess shrugged. 'I left it at home.'

'I guessed you might have done. I asked Personnel to send up another one. It should be waiting for you.'

Uneasily, she did as he requested, but completed each question with the bare minimum of detail, giving little thought to her answers. Lucy watched in silence.

The moment it was done, Jess handed it to Andrew and indicated her intention to leave.

'I'll see you on Monday, then?' His question told her he still wasn't sure of her, a state of affairs she found perversely satisfying.

'Of course she'll be here,' Lucy answered for her. 'While you were at Roundings I rang the agency and they are quite happy for her to remain with us.'

Shaking her head in despair at them both trying to organise her life, Jess wished them a good weekend and left.

Although Ruth kept her busy as usual, she found it difficult to blot out recurrent thoughts of Andrew, not to mention Lucy and the health centre, and especially whether she had done the right thing by agreeing to return on Monday.

In the beginning Lucy would have opposed her application vehemently. Now they were both urging her to take the permanent job, and while she now knew Lucy meant it, she couldn't appreciate Andrew's motives.

Was she a fool to agree? If he still believed she was as heartless as he'd suggested when he saw Larry's photo, there was no way they would ever work together comfortably.

*   *   *

She was apprehensive as nine o'clock approached on Monday morning, but she needn't have worried. They were all kept busy—Lucy with many more registrations, Andrew with a full surgery of patients, and Jess dealing with the more minor problems and also occasionally carrying out tasks requested by Andrew.

The first student he asked her to see was another fresher, who was complaining of a bewildering variety of symptoms.

When Andrew came to see if she was free, he explained all this and added, 'I think there's an element of homesickness there, but I'm certain that's not all. It's going to take time and patience to sort out which problems need our immediate attention. If you don't mind, I think you're the person to do that.'

'I don't mind, but I'm not—'

'I'm not asking you to do my job. I just want you to help him to sort out which problems he wants help with at the moment. OK? Then feed him back to me.'

When she nodded, he added, 'If you suspect something physically wrong, don't hesitate to refer him back immediately.'

'OK,' she responded, encouraged by his apparent confidence in her, 'I'll come and get him.'

'His name's Dale Waters. Here to do Business Studies.'

Jess gave the student a warm smile. 'Come across to the treatment room for a few minutes, Dale. Take a seat and I'll make us both a coffee.'

When she had done so, she pulled up her chair alongside him. 'Now, I know you've told Dr Brent already what the problems are, but could you go over them again?'

As he listed his complaints, Jess thought Andrew had understated how many there were: sore throat, nausea, stomachache, headache, no energy, acne, both on his face and shoulders, hair falling out—the list went on and on.

'When did you arrive in Bradstoke, Dale?' she asked as he paused for breath.

'Last Thursday. Mum and Dad brought me.'

'Is your home nearby?'

He shook his head. 'No. In Essex. Just about as far from here as possible.'

'So you won't get home very often during term time?'

He looked down miserably and shook his head. 'No.'

'And all these symptoms have started since you got here?'

He looked sheepish. 'Not really. I've had the problem with my skin and hair for a while now.'

Jess nodded thoughtfully. 'Have you got a room on campus?'

'No. I'm renting a room in town.'

Jess checked the address on his notes, but didn't know the area. 'Are you warm enough there?'

'There's an electric heater, but one of the other tenants told me it's expensive to run, so I haven't tried it yet.'

'What about hot water?'

'There's a heater thing in the bathroom.'

'Electric as well?'

'I think so.'

'Have you registered on your course yet?'

He nodded. 'On Friday.'

'So you've met some of the people you'll be studying with then?'

'One or two.' He seemed dubious whether that was a good thing or not. 'They all seemed to know one another and I felt like an outsider.'

'Do you think that's because you don't live on the site?'

He nodded miserably. 'I guess so.'

Jess felt as if she was ploughing through treacle, trying to get at the information she needed. Andrew had been right. This was going to take patience, and time. And there were no doubt more patients queuing to see her.

She questioned him further about his symptoms, and was surprised when he suddenly appeared to brighten and volunteered, 'You know, my headache is much better since I've been talking to you.'

Jess wondered if this was merely due to someone taking an interest in him, or if it signified something more sinister.

'What time was your registration on Friday?'

'Nine-thirty. I overslept. I only just made it in time.'

'You were tired? All day?'

'No, I don't think so.'

'What did you do at the weekend?'

'I came up here both days and watched the football. Then went to the bar.'

'Didn't you make any friends there?'

He shrugged. 'It was pretty empty.'

'Did you feel OK yesterday?'

He frowned. 'Not really. I drank too much Saturday night.'

Again feeling she was getting nowhere, Jess suggested gently, 'Why don't you go and get yourself some fresh air, and come back just before lunchtime. Then we can have a much longer chat without being disturbed.'

The next student for her attention was the hockey player whose abrasions Jess had cleaned up the previous Friday. 'I wonder if you'd check it for me? It's still painful.'

Jess removed the dressing and was pleased with what she saw. There was no sign of infection. 'It's healing well. I'm afraid shins are always more painful than the rest of the body. I'll put a dry dressing on today and in a couple of days you can expose it to the air.'

'I'm playing again Wednesday, so I'd better keep it covered then, hadn't I?'

'Definitely. Is that Wednesday evening?'

'No afternoon. Sports afternoon.'

'In that case at least one of us should be here until five-ish, so if you've any worries, let us see it.'

The hockey player left happily, and Jess was kept so busy for the remainder of the morning that she couldn't believe it when she saw Dale back in the waiting room as she showed her last patient out.

'I won't be a moment,' she told him, 'I need to complete my paperwork.'

As she filled in records for her morning's work, Andrew walked in.

'How's it going, Jess?'

'Fine. I've just finished the routine work, but I asked Dale Waters to come back again. He's in the waiting room now.'

Andrew frowned. 'You didn't get anywhere with him?'

Jess shrugged. 'I'm not sure. He said he felt better talking to me, which could mean it was because I was taking an interest in him, but—there was something about him. He actually looked brighter. Which made me wonder if there could be some disease process going on that makes him feel worse in the mornings. I questioned him about the weekend and it seemed to be the same pattern then, even though there was no one taking a particular interest in him.'

Andrew was thoughtful. 'Do you know if he's living on campus?'

'No, he's not. In a flat.'

Andrew checked his address. 'I wonder?'

'What about?'

'Carbon monoxide poisoning.'

Jess frowned. 'I did ask him about his room. He said there was an electric heater and that he thought the water heater was electric as well.'

'Let's get him in and check.'

'How do you feel now?' Andrew asked Dale once he was seated.

'Much better.'

'That's good. Did you get your flat through the accommodation office?'

Puzzled, Dale shook his head. 'No. From the paper.'

'Are you sure both the heaters are electric?'

'I'm not really sure about the water heater.'

'Let's go and see for ourselves.'

Andrew and Dale left, and Lucy had gone to lunch by the time Andrew reappeared alone.

As Jess stood up to make him a coffee he seized her round the waist and pirouetted her around the room. 'I knew we'd make a good team. It *was* a gas water heater and that lad was being poisoned. The flue had been blocked with rags to keep out the draught. The wall above and behind was heavily stained. Of course, when we found him, the landlord accused Dale of doing the blocking, but the staining was so bad it must have taken months to get that way.

'So, as there are students in some of the other rooms, I contacted our housing officer and he joined us. Under duress, the landlord has agreed to have every room in the building checked as a matter of urgency. Today, if at all possible, otherwise all the tenants will be advised to sleep elsewhere for the night, or keep all their windows open.'

'That's great.'

'And it's not all. In the meantime, Dale has been allocated a room on campus. A student gave back word this morning. He's gone to collect the key.'

'That'll make his day for him.'

'If it hadn't been for you saying how he got better during the day, we could have had a tragedy on our hands.' Andrew waltzed her around the floor again. 'You're the best diagnostic detective around.'

Jess fought to escape his hold, and succeeded in time to see Lucy standing in the doorway, watching with amazement.

Andrew turned and grinned at her. 'This miracle-worker has just sorted today's most difficult problem.'

'Not exactly,' Jess demurred.

Andrew told Lucy about it while Jess made coffee for them all. As she sipped her coffee, Jess had to admit that the morning she had been so worried about had gone well.

Andrew had a visit to do. 'It's Russell,' he explained to Jess. 'He came out of hospital yesterday.'

'Is he not going home to convalesce?'

'Not if all continues to go well. He feels he hasn't had a chance to settle into the college, or his course, and doesn't want to get behind. I think he should be OK. He seems to have made plenty of friends willing to do what they can, and he has such a positive attitude. He'll go far.'

The remainder of the week went equally well, but Jess sensed that although she and Lucy were getting on well together Andrew was handling any contact between them on an impersonal basis. So she was astounded when her belief that from now on Lucy would assist with the second surgery proved to be wrong.

'Andrew wants you to go with him to Roundings today,' the younger girl confided blithely as they drank their morning coffee on Friday. 'I want to get stuck into this paperwork.'

When she dashed off to keep a lunch date with Grant, Jess became aware that Andrew was studying her closely, as if undecided whether to broach an important topic. She felt her nerves tauten in anticipation. Larry hadn't been mentioned all week, although she was sure it couldn't last.

Nevertheless, she had begun to relax, but the way he was looking at her now made her apprehensive as she thought of the shared car journey to Roundings.

As usual he helped himself to one of her sandwiches, but didn't bite into it immediately.

'What do I owe you for feeding me?'

Jess raised her head sharply to meet his gaze. 'You don't owe me anything.'

'I can't allow you to make me a sandwich every day without some recompense.'

'I don't want anything. It's easier to make a sandwich with two slices of bread, and I often used to throw the second one away. Or eat it when I didn't really want it. For the sake of my figure, I'm grateful to you for disposing of it.'

His eyes appraised her from head to foot and he teased her gently. 'I can't believe that.'

Still far too aware of him for her own comfort, Jess felt herself blushing. 'I'll make some more coffee.' She rushed through to the treatment room and was horrified to hear him following.

'I meant it.' He didn't enlarge on what until she handed him the coffee. 'If, as seems likely, you are going to stay on here, and you won't let me pay you for the sandwiches, I must treat you at least one day a week. Perhaps we could go to the little café, like before, starting next Friday, on the way to Roundings?'

Annoyed at him suggesting it was a foregone conclusion she would continue to work there, she informed him curtly, 'I'd rather not. I get a cooked meal in the evening, so a sandwich is all I need.'

With a sigh, he returned to his seat and said impassively, 'Then I'll pay you.' Having made that decision, he dropped the subject.

Confused by her own mixed response, Jess didn't reply. She felt insulted that he thought she needed the money, and yet she appreciated him not taking her for granted. She had to admit that her heart had pounded at his suggestion they share a meal, but his ready acceptance of her refusal must surely mean that the offer had been made out of nothing more than a sense of duty.

They were *en route* to Roundings when he dropped his bombshell. 'You'll be pleased to know that your application for the temporary post has been successful. You'll hear officially next week.'

So that's what he'd been hinting at lunchtime! 'Were there no other applicants?' she asked guardedly.

'Plenty, but none with your experience.'

'You didn't interview any of them?'

He shook his head. 'No need. My mind was already made up.'

Panic gripped Jess. 'Andrew, I'm not really happy about that. You know I haven't decided yet if I want the job. I do think you might have consulted me.'

'Calm down.' He rested a hand on her knee reassuringly. 'There's no damage done. If you decide not to stay we'll draw up a short list.' He returned his hand to the gear lever.

But too late for Jess. After a week of bottling up her emotions, just his touch had been too much for her. If only she wasn't so attracted to him she could have coped. As it was, to her utter humiliation, tears cascaded down her cheeks, and she couldn't find a tissue to mop them up.

As they were nearing their destination, he pulled into the side of the road and proffered a clean handkerchief.

Jess took it gratefully, but as she sensed him distancing himself from her she couldn't help but wonder if it was because he was afraid that Sylvia might see them together. A thought which curbed her emotional turmoil immediately.

Hurriedly dabbing her eyes and blowing her nose, she turned towards him. 'Sorry about that. I'm all right now.'

He set the car back into motion. 'I didn't intend to upset you. If you don't want the job, just say so.'

Thankful that he hadn't guessed the real reason for her tears, she replied, 'I expect if you'd told me you'd given the job to someone else, I'd have reacted the same way. I'm behaving like an immature teenager. I should know what I want by this time in life, shouldn't I?' She gave a brittle laugh, hoping to convince him she saw it all as a joke.

He turned his head sharply to look at her, before returning his eyes to the road.

He parked in his usual spot and led the way down the corridor of the old building. Jess pretended to examine the ceiling mouldings, but with Andrew beside her concentrating on anything was an impossibility.

There were only a couple of students waiting at the door when they arrived, and the numbers that afternoon were a steady trickle. No way could they have called it busy.

When there was a lull in the students wanting to register, Jess tidied the cupboards and drawers, making sure all the paperwork was up-to-date and that there was nothing Andrew could fault her on.

She was pleased at the interruption when Zoe came in, wanting her to check the burnt hand was going on OK.

'How does it feel to you?'

'OK—but it feels very tight when I try to move it.'

'That's only to be expected. It'll take months to get completely back to normal, but it's healed so well, I'm sure you'll get there eventually,' she reassured her. 'Every time you wash up, or have a bath, exercise your hand in the warm water. It's easier that way.'

Zoe appeared to want to chat, and when Andrew had finished his consultation he joined them, checking with Zoe that all was well with the other girls involved in the fire.

When she left he asked Jess, 'Did you make health-check appointments for all those registering?'

Jess nodded. 'Of course. But it seems Lucy was right. Not one who had an appointment this afternoon has turned up.'

He shook his head ruefully. 'You'd better send them reminders and another appointment. And if any more register this afternoon, we'll see them right away. I'm just going for a wander. Back in ten minutes or so.'

He didn't say where he was going, and she wondered if he'd gone in search of Sylvia. Telling herself it was none of her business, she took the opportunity to make sure the drawers and cupboards in his room were tidy and well stocked.

Hearing the outer door open some time later, she emerged to find it was Andrew.

'Playing doctors?' Jess recognised a tentative return to

his good-natured banter, but nevertheless she felt she'd been caught trespassing.

An unwelcome colour rising in her cheeks, she blustered nervously, 'I was only checking your stocks. And tidying the drawers. I never saw such a mess as the left-hand one.'

He chuckled. 'Untidy brute, aren't I?'

'I didn't…'

He walked through to his room, laughing at Jess's unfinished protest. 'And now I won't be able to find anything—never can when Lucy's had a go at them.'

'Were you looking for something in particular?' she asked accusingly.

'Nothing,' he teased. 'Just making an observation.' He perched on the corner of his desk and thoughtfully watched Jess filling out the remainder of her notes. 'Aren't you curious to know where I've been?'

Without a clue as to what answer he expected, she shrugged. 'I thought you were probably looking at the burnt-out remains.'

He appeared disappointed by her lack of curiosity. 'I promised you a proper stained glass window on your first day here, and I hoped to arrange for you to see it this afternoon, but Sylvie wasn't there.'

Sylvie? His use of the pet name for the librarian he'd used to live with cut through her chest like a knife. She'd been right about where he'd been and that meant they *were* still close. Although why it should have this effect on her when she knew it already, she couldn't imagine.

'I can see it another day,' she finally managed to blurt out.

'I'll make sure you can.'

She was thankful when he suggested they lock up and return to the main site.

On the way, he asked, 'You will be back on Monday, won't you?'

She sighed deeply and nodded. 'If the agency are happy. I haven't been in contact with them yet.'

'Is there any reason why they wouldn't be?'

She shrugged. 'Not really. Unless another practice asks specifically for me.'

'And I guess that's quite likely, Jess. So, although I'm not going to press you for a decision about the job today, I think if you do contact the agency, you'd better let them know it's a possibility. I don't want you poached from under my nose.'

His earlier mention of Sylvie made her study his strong, clean profile in the hope of discovering exactly what he meant by that, but his face was impassive as he watched the road ahead.

As he parked the car, he asked, 'Have you any plans for the weekend?'

'Ruth'll keep me fully occupied until Monday.'

He nodded approvingly. 'I can imagine.' He pulled into his named parking space. 'There's no need for you to come back into the surgery today.'

'Thanks,' she murmured. 'Have a good weekend.'

As she slammed her car door closed she thought she heard him speak, but when she turned to where he'd been standing, it was to see him already striding towards the building.

CHAPTER EIGHT

JESS found it difficult to settle to anything that weekend. She knew she would have to give him an answer about the job on Monday or Tuesday, and, despite Ruth's undeniable pleasure at seeing her so often on recent evenings, she couldn't make up her mind.

She'd known from day one that she would enjoy the work, but Andrew and Lucy had both been so hostile she hadn't wanted to stay any more than they'd wanted her to. How the situation had changed in just three weeks!

Now they both wanted her to join the team and she was the one who was prevaricating. Partly due to her foolish heart refusing to accept that Andrew was nothing more than the doctor she was currently working with, but mainly because she was sure he must still be brooding about Larry. If she stayed, some time she was going to have to explain what had happened all those years ago.

She telephoned the agency early on Monday morning. 'Bradstoke College want me to stay for another week, and perhaps permanently. I'll let you know as soon as a decision is made.'

The manager was surprised. 'I thought it was only a temporary job they had on offer?'

'Officially it is, but Dr Brent seems to think it'll be permanent.'

'Think carefully, Jess. You've been on our books for a long time, and we try and offer you the best positions.'

'I know. That's why I'm not prepared to make the decision lightly. I'll wait until I know something definite.'

After dropping Ruth at the school gates, she made her

way to the health centre, wondering what the morning would bring.

Andrew greeted her with a smile. 'Welcome back aboard. Here's the official job offer.' He handed her an envelope and smiled towards Lucy. 'By the way, I'm still trying to get both salaries upgraded.'

'Thanks.' Jess didn't know what else to say.

Andrew made it easy for her. 'You remember Tom Steel? He's being discharged today.'

'Will you have to see him?'

'No. He has a local GP so we won't be involved.'

'I'm glad to hear he's done so well.'

Andrew nodded. 'Thanks to you.'

Embarrassed, she murmured with a laugh, 'I think you had something to do with it, too.'

Lucy went to Roundings with Andrew that afternoon, and all went so well for the next couple of days that when, on Wednesday, he told Jess he had managed to get both their salaries increased, and that Joanne had sent in her resignation, she agreed to accept the permanent post that was offered.

The moment she told him of her decision, she sensed his attitude towards her subtly changing. Although he didn't exactly probe for information, whenever they were alone together he tried to turn the conversation to her life with Ruth.

Over their lunchtime sandwich on Thursday, he murmured, 'Now you're going to be here regularly, I'll make other arrangements for my lunch. I guess you have to get up quite early enough, without making sandwiches for me. It must be a rush to get Ruth to school and be here by nine.'

'As I said before, it's no problem. I'd be doing it for myself anyway.'

'So what time do you have to get up?'

She shrugged. 'Around seven—certainly no earlier.'

'So will you change your mind about coming for a meal some Friday lunchtimes?'

'I'd rather not, thanks. As I said, I prefer my cooked meal in the evening.'

He sighed deeply. 'One evening, then? Larry's parents would babysit, wouldn't they?'

'Yes. They're happy to do that occasionally, but—'

'But you're not happy to leave her! Do you *ever* get out without Ruth in tow, apart from when you're at work?'

When she didn't answer immediately, he nodded and said, 'I thought not. You should make a life for yourself.'

'There'll be time enough for that when Ruth's older.'

He shook his head despairingly and, moving towards her, placed a hand on her shoulder. 'It could be too late then.'

Raising her eyes to search his face, she experienced a crushing tightness in her chest as she read the tender concern in his expression.

In that instant she recognised that the awareness that had flared between them when they first met had not, as she'd tried to tell herself, been extinguished the night Andrew had learnt that Larry was Ruth's father. Her foolish heart had been right all along.

'Jess, I—'

The waiting room door opened at that moment to admit Lucy, so Andrew swiftly removed his hand from her shoulder, and, although she hadn't known she was holding it, Jess felt the breath leave her body in a great rush.

She didn't know whether to be grateful or disappointed by Lucy's interruption, especially when the flow of students with appointments for health-checks denied them any opportunity for further discussion.

She left at her normal time, leaving Lucy and Andrew to complete the afternoon's work, but that evening, for the first time ever, she found it difficult to put Ruth first in her thoughts. Instead, she tried hopelessly to imagine what Andrew had been about to say when he was interrupted by Lucy's arrival.

After a busy Friday morning surgery, which ran on into the lunch-hour, the first chance she had to speak with Andrew about anything but work was in the car *en route* to Roundings.

To her disappointment, Andrew was preoccupied with the unusually heavy traffic, and barely spoke apart from asking rhetorically, 'I wonder what caused such a snarl-up today?'

The surgery was busier than she'd ever known it, and when she checked her watch, Jess was amazed to discover it was way after four. Not expecting any more consultations that afternoon, she was about to lock the door when Zoe came in.

'Problem?' Jess asked.

'Not really. More of a chat. I don't really know who else to talk to. I'm just worried because, although it's supposed to be out of bounds, a couple of the lads keep mucking around in the burnt-out building, trying to frighten us girls as it gets dark.'

'Have you told the warden?'

Zoe shook her head. 'I hadn't thought of her.'

'I should think Rachel would be the person to deal with them. I presume you know who they are?'

Zoe nodded ruefully. 'I think they're the same two who are in trouble for fooling about when the fire started, so I suppose they think they've nothing to lose.'

Jess was surprised. 'You mean the fire was their fault?'

Zoe shrugged. 'I don't think it's been proved, but they are certainly suspects. And they know it.'

'In that case I think you should definitely tell the warden what they're up to, so that she can take whatever steps are necessary.'

Zoe nodded. 'I'll see if I can find her before I go home for the weekend.'

When Andrew's last patient left, he told Jess, 'We're running late for your treat.'

'What?'

'I've arranged for you to see the old chapel window. It's hidden in the librarian's den at the back.'

It gave her a warm feeling to know that he'd taken the trouble, but his next statement promptly dampened her excitement. 'Sylvia has promised to wait around until we get up there today.'

'That's kind of her.' Struggling to remain calm, she locked the drawers and cupboards, then murmured, 'We've been busy today. What happens if anyone is taken ill on the days we aren't here?'

'There are plenty of first-aiders, or they call me out. It's never caused a problem.'

They climbed the flight of stone stairs to the old chapel and Andrew introduced her to the head librarian, a woman about Jess's own age. 'This is Sylvia—she says you can go straight through.'

Jess felt dowdy in her uniform beside the chic of his ex-live-in partner. As Lucy had said, Sylvia was certainly blonde and beautiful, and, watching the darting eyes take in every detail of Jess, she could believe in the brains.

Wondering if Sylvia had made a special effort because Andrew had said they were coming, or whether she always dressed so smartly, Jess's greeting was wary.

'It's through that door at the bottom,' Andrew directed. 'I'll wait here as there's not much room.'

With Sylvia! Who obviously knew Andrew very well indeed!

Jess wished they hadn't come, when, peering at some of the more inaccessible bits of architecture, partly hidden by boxes and piles of books, she overheard Andrew asking about friends they obviously had in common.

She'd only just managed to clear a good view of the partly hidden window when he came in search of her, checking his watch.

'Is it time we were off?' she asked, her eyes fixed firmly on the stained glass.

'I don't want to make Lucy late leaving,' he replied.

Her eyes alight with interest, Jess turned reluctantly. 'OK. Let's go. I'm pleased to have seen it. I would never have guessed it existed.'

'Now you know where it is, perhaps you could come and examine it in detail another day, Jess?' Sylvia had come up behind them and made the offer readily.

Surprised by the friendly offer, Jess smiled gratefully. 'I'd like to do that, and perhaps take a couple of photographs.'

'Are you free tomorrow?' The librarian was locking the massive door behind her. 'I'll be in on my own in the afternoon, so you can spend as much time as you like.'

Jess hadn't intended bothering any more with the window, but, noting what appeared to be a flash of anxiety in Andrew's eyes, she wondered if he was trying to rush her away because she and Sylvia were getting on too well!

Knowing that Gwen didn't mind looking after Ruth on the odd Saturday, she accepted the offer with alacrity. 'That'd be great.'

As Andrew had taken a keen interest in the arrangements, she wasn't too surprised when on their return journey he asked, 'You liked Sylvia, did you?'

Aware she hadn't expected such an instant rapport with the girl, Jess nodded. 'She seems nice.'

'Don't believe all she tells you, will you?'

Jess looked at him in bewilderment. 'About the window?'

He laughed drily. 'Sylvia used to be on the main site. I know her well.'

'Ye-es?' prompted Jess, wondering why he was telling her this now.

'I'll spell it out for you before she does. We lived together for a couple of years. Split up last February, which is why I'm not making much of a success of living alone.'

Although her heart leapt at his words, she couldn't help wondering if he was telling the whole truth, or if there was still something between them. 'So? I don't see that's any more my business than Larry is yours.'

'You don't?' He seemed disappointed by her lack of interest, but, as he'd already brought his car to a stop in the car park, she opted not to return to the surgery but transferred directly to her own car.

Driving home, she knew that it was his obvious anxiety about her meeting with Sylvia that was making her all the more determined to keep the appointment. He had condemned her without knowing the true facts about her life with Larry. It would be interesting to hear what Sylvia had to say about Andrew's part in *their* relationship.

It was somebody or other's law that the next day was the one Saturday that Gwen and Les had arranged to go out with friends.

'It doesn't matter,' Jess reassured a distraught Gwen that evening. 'I can rearrange the visit.'

'You go out so rarely. It'd be nice for you to make a friend your own age.'

'If I wanted a hectic social life, I've plenty of contacts, Gwen. There's time for that in the future.'

She rang the Roundings site, but Sylvia had left for the day and would not be in until the following afternoon.

She left a message cancelling her visit, intending to contact the librarian the following week. However, the next morning her new friend rang and said to bring Ruth. 'I'd like to meet her.'

Jess got them both ready, and they arrived in time to have a cup of tea with Sylvia, who had thoughtfully provided biscuits and orange squash for Ruth.

The library was empty, so while Jess went to take photographs of the window, Sylvia attempted to entertain Ruth by showing her the layout of the books. Having left the door open, Jess was conscious that the librarian wasn't getting many answers from Ruth. She had just made up her mind to spare the poor woman any more embarrassment and take Ruth home, when she heard footsteps entering the library.

'Hello? Anybody there?' Jess couldn't mistake the deep brown tones of Andrew's voice.

Holding her breath, she heard Sylvia's answering, 'Hi,' then cringed as Ruth's childish voice piped up.

'Have you come to read me another story?'

Jess hurried out before he could answer. 'What are you doing here?'

'I was called out to see a student with stomachache, so I thought I might as well see if you were still here.'

Sensing it wasn't the whole truth, Jess enquired sceptically, 'What's the matter with the student?'

'I've left him to Rachel's tender care. That'll do more for him than anything I might prescribe.' He smiled down at Ruth. 'I didn't realise you were bringing this little charmer.'

'Gwen and Les were busy,' Jess informed him curtly. Sure now that this wasn't a chance meeting, and fearing subconsciously that Ruth would pester him further, she wanted to run for home. 'Actually, we were just leaving.'

'But you haven't been here long.' The surprise in Sylvia's voice appeared to spur Andrew into action.

'Shall we go for a walk round the grounds, Ruth, and let Mummy look at this window in peace?' He took her small hand in his. 'If we're lucky we'll find a couple of horses in a field at the back.'

'Ooh! Yes, please.' Ruth was already tugging him towards the entrance.

Jess tried to say they must leave, but neither Ruth nor Andrew were listening.

'See you later,' he called over his shoulder as they departed from view.

Sylvia smiled nervously at Jess. 'I'm not much good with children. I don't really like them and they seem to sense it.'

Jess shrugged. 'Ruth seemed happy enough with you,

and I'd just about finished making notes. I just want to take a few photographs.' She hesitated, then blurted out what was on her mind, 'Andrew's visit was planned, wasn't it?'

The challenge hung in the air between them until Sylvia nodded slowly. 'He rang earlier and I said you were bringing Ruth.' She hesitated, before continuing unhappily, 'Has he told you why we split up?'

Jess shook her head. 'It's really none of my business.'

'Do you want more children?'

'I—I haven't thought about it.' She was so taken aback by the directness of Sylvia's question that she stuttered her reply. 'I—I have nothing more than a working relationship with Andrew, you know.'

'He gets on well with your daughter, though?'

Jess's musing reply was barely audible. 'She's only seen him a couple of times before today, and then only briefly.'

Sylvia's eyebrow lifted with surprise. 'You must have noticed how good he is with children, though?'

Jess sensed Sylvia was leading up to something, but, puzzled as to what it might be, she murmured, 'I really haven't had much opportunity.'

'Andrew and I split because he desperately wants a family and I don't. I think that's partly why he's come today. He knew I'd be out of my depth.'

Reading between the lines, Jess said slowly, 'If you're suggesting he sees Ruth as a ready-made family, I'm sure you're mistaken.'

Sylvia smiled wryly. 'I shouldn't be too sure. Jess, I've known Andrew much longer than you. Long enough to be pretty sure that you're wrong. It's Ruth he's interested in.'

Ruth. Had she herself been just a means to cultivate Ruth's friendship? Jess was stunned. Was that why he'd offered her the job? Why he'd tried to turn the conversation so often to talk about Ruth?

Anger at his having made such a fool of her made Jess's eyes sparkle as she asked Sylvia, 'Did he ask you to talk to me?'

The librarian looked shifty.

'He did.' Jess answered herself. 'Why?'

'He didn't ask me to in so many words, but he suggested that, as we seemed to get on well together, I befriend you and try to get you away from your boring existence.'

'But it's what I want,' Jess protested hotly. 'Ruth's my life and—'

'Exactly,' Sylvia broke in. 'Andrew's worried about what'll happen when she grows up, which will be all too soon.'

The silence that followed hung between them. Jess too incensed to argue, and Sylvia scared that she had said too much.

'Jess, he cares about you—cares enough to go to all this trouble.'

Jess's eyes took on a steely glint as she replied, 'Thank you, Sylvia. You've made it all very clear. Andrew doesn't give a damn about me. He's only concerned about what happens to Ruth. I should have realised it long ago. The first and only time he came to the house he timed his visit for Ruth's bedtime. Thank you again. I've been very stupid, but now I understand, I can deal with the situation.'

Fuming at his interference in their life, she crashed through the library doors and, ignoring Sylvia's anguished cry of, 'Jess,' rushed out in search of her daughter, determined she shouldn't stay with Andrew a moment longer. The more time they spent together, the more Ruth would resent being separated from him.

It was some time before she found them, behind the fire-damaged hall of residence.

Ruth was balanced precariously on the narrow boundary wall, attempting to pat the heads of two brown and white ponies who were unimpressed by her attention. Andrew was too intent on holding firmly onto Ruth to hear Jess's approach.

'I'll take Ruth now. We have to go.' Dismissing as futile all the recriminations she had dredged up as she stalked round the site, Jess snatched Ruth from the wall and without a word set off in the direction of the car park.

'Jess!' Andrew gasped in surprise. 'Hang on a minute.'

Ignoring him, she bundled Ruth into the car and, without belting her in properly, set off towards the site exit.

As the car ran in front of the burnt-out shell of the students' residence, she heard a scream and an urgent cry of warning. Looking up, she saw the top part of the building crumbling before her eyes. Instinctively aware that she couldn't get the car away fast enough, she snatched a snivelling Ruth for the second time in as many minutes, and ran out onto the grass-covered quadrangle.

As she crushed Ruth anxiously to her, a couple of blood-curdling screams tore through the air to be followed by a prolonged rumble and then silence. The taste of brick dust invaded her mouth as she tried to stop herself trembling. She must go and see if anyone was hurt, but she couldn't leave Ruth.

She looked around frantically, thankfully spotting a familiar face rushing towards her. 'Look after Ruth, Sylvia. I think someone needs help.'

Giving the librarian no chance to refuse, Jess rushed towards the debris, dreading what she was going to find.

As she reached the collapsed wall she saw Andrew, scrabbling away frantically at the rubble covering her flattened car. 'Jess! Ruth! Jess! Can you hear me?'

Of course. He had been round at the back of the building and hadn't seen their escape. She gently touched his arm. 'Andrew.' When her voice didn't immediately register with him, she moved closer and repeated his name, louder this time. 'Andrew.' As he turned his head towards her she was surprised by the frank despair in his dark eyes, which initially didn't register who she was.

'I must get them out. They're not answering.' He turned his attention back to the remains of the vehicle.

'Andrew,' she said again, grasping his arm firmly this time. 'Come away. We got out before the wall fell. Thank

God I hadn't fastened our seat belts. Ruth is over there with Sylvia.'

It was still quite a few seconds before he took in what she was saying. When he did, he clung to her as if he couldn't believe it was really her. 'Why—why in God's name didn't they make this building safe?'

Enjoying the novelty of being in his arms, she clung to him, until Andrew said quietly, 'I think we're needed, Jess. Someone is screaming.'

'This is all my fault. *I* should have told the warden,' she wailed, as they made their way carefully forward.

'We'll apportion blame later, love,' he told her gently.

At the edge of the area of debris, they tracked down the screams. At first they could see nothing, then Jess peered through a crack and saw a student trying to free her legs, which were trapped by one of the stone door supports. The girl must have been running away when the pillar fell, and, though more rubble had crashed down, the upper parts of her body had been shielded by the remains of the door itself.

'Hello. I'm the college nurse.' Jess waited for some sign that the girl had heard her.

When none was forthcoming Andrew shouted loudly as he could. 'Hello? Can you hear me?'

The girl answered this time. 'I can't move my legs—do something, please.' Her sobbing voice rose rapidly to a note of panic. 'I can't move. It's my legs. Get me out, can't you? Get me out before more of it falls.'

'Try to keep calm, love. Are you alone?' Jess couldn't see any sign of others, but she wanted to be sure.

The girl shrieked her answer. 'Of course I'm alone. Get me out of here.'

Jess looked towards Andrew, who was frantically searching through the rubble to discover a way to reach the girl without dislodging further stones.

He shook his head. 'It's going to be a long job. We'll have to move carefully if we're not to make matters worse.'

Some of the other students were already scrabbling away at the edges of the debris. Andrew went over to join them.

'Look, lads—we must work together. Otherwise we'll put the girl's life in jeopardy. We need to work out a strategy.'

Sirens in the distance heralded the welcome arrival of fire-engines and ambulances.

He returned to where the girl could hear best. 'Reinforcements are here. It shouldn't take too long now. What's your name?'

The girl tried to stifle her renewed sobs. 'Mary. Mary Pointer.'

'All right, Mary. The men are going to have to move the rubble covering you brick by brick—it'll take time. But as long as they're careful there's no danger of a further fall. The firemen'll know the best way to go about it. Now, tell me, do your legs hurt?'

Mary burst into floods of tears again. 'The left one does. I—I can't bear it much longer.'

Andrew turned to Jess and a burly ambulanceman who had joined her. 'She needs painkillers if we're going to prevent shock developing.'

'Could be a problem,' the ambulanceman warned pessimistically.

Andrew turned to Jess. 'I've morphine in my bag. I'll get it from the car.' He ran off, leaving Jess to chat with Mary, in an attempt to take her mind off her dangerous predicament.

'How am I going to reach her?' he asked on his return.

They all tried to figure out the best approach. Jess pointed to a narrow opening beneath one part of the heavy stone. 'Under there, I should think.'

'It's too small. You'll never do it, sir.' The ambulanceman was clearly a pessimist.

'The doctor may not be able to, but I can.' Jess divested herself of her suede jacket and lay down, intending to wriggle under the stone.

'You are not doing it.' Andrew pulled her up again. 'It could be dangerous.'

'I'm slighter, though.'

'Maybe, but it's too risky, Jess. You have your daughter to think of. You could get hurt as well if we dislodge the fragile balance.'

Jess looked round at the ambulanceman, but his size was definitely against him.

'I'll do it,' Andrew told her. 'I've long arms and should be able to reach her easily. Here, take my bag and hand me the drugs once I'm in position.'

Without listening to further argument, he squeezed himself into the narrow opening.

After wriggling slowly towards Mary, he called, 'Hand me the syringe of painkiller, Jess.'

She did as she was asked, but then heard him swear. His shoulders were too broad to go through the last narrow opening.

Jess could hear him reassuring Mary and then she heard him shout, 'I'm coming out.'

He handed Jess the syringe while the ambulanceman helped him out of the opening. 'If I force my way through it could make matters worse.

'There must be some way we can get to her.'

'I'll do it,' Jess told him quietly. 'It must be safe as far as you went, and I'm sure I can get through that last gap with no problem. Please let me try.'

Andrew reluctantly agreed. 'But don't take any risks, Jess. As long as you do exactly what I did, it should be OK.'

Once Andrew had handed her the painkiller, Jess wriggled gradually towards Mary, trying all the while to despatch the fear that was scurrying round in her brain, and to ignore the way the bare skin on her arms and legs was being painfully abraded as she fought her way through the narrowest points.

At length she reached a spot where she could touch

Mary, and the girl looked at her with eyes still wet with tears.

Jess checked the student's pulse, asking, 'Did you hit your head at all, Mary?'

'No, it was just my legs. Why?' She was scared.

Jess smiled reassuringly up at the girl from her prone position. 'It's just that this painkiller would mask any symptoms of head injury. If there's no risk of that I can make you more comfortable.'

'All right, Jess?' Andrew's worried whisper reached her ears as she administered the injection.

'Fine, Andrew. We're both fine.'

'They're moving the stones quickly now—it shouldn't be long.'

Mary was soon calmer and rested her head back on the ground behind her, eventually dropping into a fitful doze.

Jess allowed herself to relax slightly, but couldn't put thoughts of Ruth from her mind. What if the remaining structure should fall and kill her? Would Ruth ever get over the loss of her only parent? The thought filled her mind when she wasn't checking on Mary's condition, but she knew she had to remain where she was.

She was startled when one of the firemen lifted a large piece of stone away, revealing the presence of their rescuers.

Within a short time the stone doorpost was carefully raised by the firemen, using lifting equipment. The moment Mary was released from her imprisonment, Andrew and the ambulancemen checked her condition and tried to prevent complications arising later by stabilising her damaged leg with an inflatable splint, which also restricted any outpouring of plasma into the crushed tissues.

As soon as possible, she was loaded into the ambulance for a thorough check on her overall condition.

'You'd better come to the hospital, too.' The ambulance driver addressed Jess urgently. 'Those grazes look nasty.'

She shook her head. 'I must get back to my daughter. She must be scared out of her wits.'

The moment the ambulance sped away with Mary, Andrew turned his attention to Jess. 'Thank you, love.' He leant towards her and kissed her gently. 'I'd hug you, but I might hurt you. Those abrasions need looking at.'

'I'll see to them. After I've checked Ruth's all right.'

Andrew followed her across to where Sylvia was cuddling Ruth to her as if it was the most natural thing in the world.

'Mummy!' The little girl flung herself against Jess, making her wince, although she didn't allow Ruth to see it.

Andrew stood by silently for a few moments, then, after thanking Sylvia and telling her she was clearly a natural with children after all, he said quietly to Jess, 'No argument, now. I'm going to run you to the hospital. Ruth can come with us. I'll stay with her while they sort out those cuts.'

CHAPTER NINE

'I'LL be all right.'

Andrew's eyes were moist as he murmured, 'When you leave the hospital you will be, come on.' He swung Ruth up into his arms and, watching him, Jess recalled what Sylvia had told her earlier. She almost regretted accepting his offer of transport, though what else she could have done now her car was crushed, she couldn't think.

It was two hours before she was released from the dressing area, and she found Ruth sound asleep on Andrew's lap.

The nurse who accompanied her indicated them in the corner with a nod of her head. 'Her father soon quietened her down.'

Andrew heard the comment but merely grinned as he rose unsteadily to his feet, hampered by the small burden. 'That looks better. How's Mary?'

'They've taken her to the admission ward. I've got her home number here. I said we would ring her parents. She thought they'd be terrified if someone from the hospital rang.'

Andrew nodded. 'I can easily do that.'

He opened the back door of his Granada and indicated that Jess should climb in. Then he placed Ruth carefully on the seat beside her, pillowing her head on Jess's arm. As he secured both seat belts, he murmured, 'I'll take it slowly.'

They arrived back at Luccombe Gardens to find the house still empty. Jess was surprised. It seemed so long since she'd left home with Ruth to look at the library window that she thought it must be the middle of the night.

Andrew dashed round and lifted Ruth out of the car. Jess searched for her keys and then with a sinking feeling, realised they were still in the flattened car.

She looked at Andrew, appalled. 'My keys. They're in the car.' After everything that had happened it was just too much, and she burst into tears.

Andrew sat the now awake Ruth in the front of the car, and cradled Jess as if she herself was a child. 'It'll be all right, don't worry.' He leant forward and kissed her hair.

'Why's Mummy crying?' Ruth asked with interest.

'Because,' he told her gently, 'your car is broken and she can't get into the house without the keys that are in it.'

'Oh.'

'We'll go round to my flat.' He released Jess slowly, then took a diary from his pocket and tore out a page. 'I'll pop a note through the door saying where we are, then Gwen and Les won't be worried. They may have heard something about the accident on a news bulletin.'

'It was all my fault.'

'What do you mean, your fault?'

'Zoe told me on Friday that a couple of lads were fooling about in that building. I told her to tell the warden. I guess she didn't bother before she went home for the weekend. If I'd done something about it myself, the collapse might never have happened.' Jess burst into tears again.

Andrew drew her to him. 'Of course it's not your fault. Come on. You're the one who's shocked now. Let's get you home as soon as we can.'

Jess numbly watched him slip the note through the door. She hadn't the energy to dispute the arrangements even if she'd wanted to. And at that moment she didn't. She wanted to be taken care of. Just for once. Let somebody else make the decisions.

When they entered his flat she was momentarily startled by the organised chaos. The varied reading matter scattered on every available surface contrasted markedly with the elegant antique furniture gracing the airy room. And yet Jess sensed how sterile the environment would be if everything was in its proper place.

Andrew rushed ahead to clear a space on the settee for Ruth, who was asleep again. 'I told you I wasn't making much of a success of living alone.'

She shook her head. 'The books are your companions. They are where they belong.'

Andrew smiled appreciatively. 'I should have known you'd excuse the mess charitably. Sit yourself down and I'll make the spare bed up for Ruth.' He made his way to one of the rooms across the hall, leaving Jess to luxuriate in the warm depths of a comfortable armchair. After the trauma of the afternoon, the warm, masculine ambience of Andrew's flat soothed her like a drug. She felt her eyelids drooping and her thoughts drifted off into a limbo where Andrew reappeared fleetingly to spirit Ruth away.

The fear that had dogged her all afternoon jolted Jess back to a frantic consciousness. Sylvia had said Andrew's only interest in Jess was to get to know Ruth better. She must take her home. Immediately. Andrew met her in the hall and, gently taking her arm, steered her back whence she had come.

He said quietly, 'She's only across the hall. She didn't wake. She'll probably sleep until morning.'

'But—but she hasn't eaten. She must be starving.'

He grinned. 'You'd never forgive me if you knew the junk food I foraged for at the hospital. But I have to report she enjoyed every mouthful of it.'

Despite herself, Jess laughed.

'That's better. Now, how are we going to revive you? A brandy? Or food?' Seating himself on the arm of her chair, he leaned forward and lightly brushed her hair with his lips. 'You tell me what you want and I'll tell you if it's possible.' In her soporific state, Jess raised her face to meet his gaze, and, as if it were the most natural thing in the world, their lips met.

Jess was lost. His seductive offer had prompted such a

state of desire that she could refuse him nothing. When he lifted her bodily so that he could slide onto the chair beneath her, she made no attempt to resist. She clung to him as if it was where she belonged and she didn't care who knew it. 'Jess,' he whispered throatily as his hands moved round to cradle her erect nipples. 'Oh, Jess. I've waited so long for this.'

Suddenly conscious that he must be aware of them straining towards him, she felt a sense of shame at her abandoned response. Suppose Ruth had woken and seen them?

The thought of Ruth brought Jess completely to her senses. She grasped his hands and roughly pushed them away. Irrationally she told herself he didn't care about her. She was just a means to an end and that end was Ruth.

Andrew groaned and cupped her cheeks with the palms of his hands. His dark eyes pierced her gaze like slivers of slate as he pleaded huskily, 'Don't stop me, Jess. You know it's right.'

Fully in control of the situation now, Jess pulled herself from his grasp and moved right away.

'Jess.' His cry was anguished.

'I'm sorry, Andrew. I must go.'

He strode across the room and into the kitchen, banging a couple of cupboard doors as if searching for something. Jess guessed he needed time to compose himself.

She settled herself back in the armchair until he returned. 'I'm sorry, Andrew. I shouldn't have come here.'

He shrugged, as if everything that had gone before was unimportant. 'I can make you an omelette. Would that do?' He made the offer dispassionately.

Devastated that a thoughtless few moments could wreak such havoc within them both, Jess felt tears pricking at the back of her eyes.

Recalling he usually went out for his meals, she guessed he had little in the larder. 'I'd love a glass of wine. Red, preferably. Nothing stronger and nothing to eat, thanks. Gwen'll cook me something when I get home.'

The telephone's clamour silenced the protest Jess sensed springing to his lips.

He lifted the receiver, and by his replies she recognised it was Gwen at the other end.

'I'll ask her, Mrs Halton.'

He pushed the 'mute' button to prevent the caller hearing his conversation. 'It's Gwen. She wants to know if you're staying here with Ruth or going back to Luccombe Gardens.' He made the statement prosaically.

'I can't stay the night here. I must get home. And I'll take Ruth with me.'

Andrew shrugged. 'After the day Ruth's had it would be criminal to disturb her now she's settled. But if *you* insist on leaving, I can look after her.' He left her in no doubt what his opinion would be if she dared to move Ruth. 'I'll bring her over to you in the morning.'

Jess felt cold inside. That was the last thing she wanted. Hadn't all this happened because she was trying to keep them apart?

Tired and confused, she shook her head, unable to come to a decision.

'What shall I tell Gwen, then?' he prompted impatiently. 'That you're coming home in a taxi? Now?'

Still struggling within herself, Jess covered her face with her hands. What option had she? 'Tell her I'm staying here,' she mumbled.

She watched through her fingers as he returned to the telephone. She had given the answer he wanted. His satisfaction was obvious as he passed on her decision.

Groaning inwardly, she resolved to sleep in with Ruth. On the floor if necessary.

Replacing the receiver, he murmured, 'Omelette it shall be, then,' and set off towards the kitchen.

'I'll do it.' Anything to push her thoughts to the back of her mind.

He shook his head. 'No way. I brought you here for some TLC.'

Guiltily she remembered his panic when he'd thought they were in the flattened car, and the care he had taken of both Ruth and herself once the drama of freeing the student was over.

Was she being selfish rejecting him in this way? Was she just afraid of releasing the emotions she had dammed up for so long, and even more afraid of sharing with anyone the pleasure her daughter brought her? Or was she right in believing his attention was solely for Ruth's benefit. Could she possibly trust him after what Sylvia had told her that afternoon?

He came through and handed her a glass of wine. 'Feeling better?'

He sipped his own wine, gazing at her with a compassion that undermined all her resolve and sent a heated tide of blood rushing back into her cheeks.

'I shouldn't have pressured you,' he said at last.

'It's just that—'

'No need for explanations, Jess. You've had one hell of a day and I'd no right to expect—'

Jess was the one to interrupt this time. 'Can't we just forget it ever happened?' If he agreed, it would make it much easier to distance herself from him.

He gave her a long, hard stare. 'I'm afraid, love, that won't be possible. For me at least. But,' he hastened to add when she was about to protest, 'and it's a big "but", I promise not to refer to it again this evening.' He placed his glass beside hers and crossed to the telephone.

'Supper won't be long, but first I must ring Mary's parents.'

Half listening to his compassionate handling of the difficult call, Jess found her eyelids drooping uncontrollably.

The next thing she knew was Andrew gently touching her arm. She started awake to discover a small table in front of her, set with an embroidered cloth and flowers. A side salad and a bread roll rested one on either side of the place setting. Without a word he hurried away, to reappear moments later with the most deliciously fluffy omelette she could remember seeing for a long time.

As he set the plate in front of her, the aroma sent her tastebuds into an ecstatic anticipation of the food she was about to eat.

'This looks delicious.' She sampled a small portion and grinned appreciatively. 'And tastes even more so.'

He settled on the settee with his own supper, obviously well satisfied by her compliments.

'I can't believe you're not making a success of living alone,' she teased. 'If this is the standard of your cooking.'

'This is my sole *chef-d'oeuvre*. Served daily, its attraction rapidly pales!'

'I can imagine.' Jess felt sufficiently relaxed now to safely join in his banter.

They enjoyed the remainder of the meal in a companionable silence.

'Coffee?' he asked as he collected together the plates. 'Sorry there's no sumptuous dessert.'

'That was fine, Andrew, and, yes, a cup of coffee would be wonderful. I'll wash up while you make it.'

'No need. I have a dishwasher.'

'Lucky you.' As he brewed the coffee she contemplated the circumstances that gave a well-equipped kitchen to someone who didn't cook while poor Gwen made delicious meals for them all with few labour-saving devices. By the time he brought the coffee through, she was asking herself if there was a moral there somewhere.

'Why the frown?' he placed the coffee in front of her and settled on the rug at her feet.

'I was pondering on the unfairness of life.'

'Why so serious all of a sudden?' He pulled his knees up to his chin, arms clasped around his long legs.

'I don't think I was being serious. It was your mention of a dishwasher. I was wondering what you did with it if you eat out all the time.'

'Good question. But you can figure it out for yourself while I make up your bed.'

'I can sleep in with Ruth. I'll be all right on her floor,' she assured him hurriedly. 'Don't worry about a bed.'

He sighed with exasperation. 'You are not sleeping on any floor after what you've been through. *This* is a sofa-bed.' He indicated the settee. '*You* will have my bed and I'll sleep on that. It's very comfortable, so stop arguing.'

He disappeared into the main bedroom and, feeling guilty at the disruption she was causing, she followed.

'Let me do the bed,' she offered, whilst making a rapid assessment of his bedroom. It wasn't the masculine strong-hold she had expected. She detected Sylvia's hand in the chintz curtains and matching bedspread, not to mention the toning wallpaper that diffused a peaceful aura within the room.

'You are the most infuriatingly independent girl I've ever met.'

Surprised by his response, Jess found herself colouring hotly. 'I'm sorry. I only wanted to help.'

'And I'm only trying to look after you and...' His voice tailed off as he searched for the right words. 'Go and sit down,' he ordered.

Uncomfortable at his intense scrutiny, she did as she was told and made her way back to the refuge of her armchair.

Years of repressing her emotions had not prepared her for this. Especially when his behaviour repeatedly changed with his current perception of her mood. He definitely wasn't as insensitive as she had first suspected!

He joined her almost immediately, dropping pillows and duvet onto the beige carpet to await conversion of the settee to a bed.

Resuming his position on the oriental rug at her feet, he gazed up into her face, his eyes searching relentlessly. 'Why are you so afraid of anyone helping you, I wonder?'

Frantically trying to resist the urge to brush an errant dark curl from his forehead, Jess started nervously.

'I—I'm not afraid. It's just…'

'Ye-es?' he prompted lazily as Jess hesitated.

Aware she must appear ungrateful, she attempted to prove otherwise. 'You've got it all wrong, Andrew. I'm more than grateful for the help Gwen and Les give me. I couldn't manage without it.'

He wasn't going to let her get away with that. 'But you're not prepared to allow anyone else a share in caring for Ruth. Why?'

Jess swallowed hard. The past few years had been anything but easy, but she had coped. The last thing she needed now was someone telling her how to bring up her daughter. 'She's doing very well at school.'

He smiled at her defence. 'I'm sure she is. It's her mother I'm worried about.'

'There's no need to be,' she retorted spiritedly. 'I'm more than content.'

'But what about Ruth? She might not know what she's missing at the moment, but one day she will. And then you'll regret the lost opportunity.'

'You're talking in riddles. Ruth has all she needs.' Wary of his ability to see the loneliness she was expert at hiding from everyone else, Jess tried to end the conversation. 'I'm very tired, Andrew. If you don't mind, I'd like to get to bed.' Sliding out of the depths of the armchair, she prepared for escape.

He nodded. 'I thought you might run for cover.' Then, with a barely perceptible change of tone, he gestured politely towards the bathroom. 'The facilities are at your disposal. Plenty of hot water. Soap and towel in your room.'

Thrown by his sudden impassivity, Jess scurried to her bedroom and closed the door. Several deep breaths later she opened the door a crack, and, hearing him crashing around in the kitchen, crossed to the bathroom.

Cursing her lack of a change of clothes, she slipped on the blue towelling robe hanging on the back of the door. Immediately she was conscious of her body heat reviving a subtle hint of Andrew's aftershave, evoking emotions that sent her heart hammering against her ribs.

She emerged to find him watching her from the depths of the armchair. 'Goodnight, Jess. Sleep well. Give me a shout if you need anything.'

Thankful that he remained where he was, she replied, 'Goodnight, Andrew, and thank you. Have a comfortable night.'

'You bet.' A teasing smile accompanied his reply, but Jess didn't wait to hear more. She closed the bedroom door firmly behind her and, slipping off the dressing gown, slid naked between the silky sheets of Andrew's bed.

Despite her jumbled thoughts, the events of the day had exhausted her. She slept the moment her head touched the pillow.

Andrew contemplated the closed door silently for several long moments, then, sighing deeply, he made his way across to the bathroom.

Remembering his robe gracing Jess's body as she raced to his bed, he grinned hugely as he imagined her reaction should she discover him in his underpants next morning.

A long, hot shower revived his aching limbs, but the disturbing thoughts of Jess were not so easy to deal with.

Despite their surface pleasantries, he felt they were further apart than on the day they'd met. True, when he'd learnt about Larry he'd flipped, and, though he'd realised almost immediately he must be wrong, the damage was done.

After what she'd been through he'd expected to need patience, but he certainly hadn't been prepared for a retreat on her part. Aware of how easily the child of a previous relationship could sour a new one, he'd thought she would be pleased by his interest in Ruth. Instead, it seemed that each small advance in his friendship with Ruth resulted in her mother taking a backward step.

A state of affairs that was hard to understand when he could sense her body's strong attraction towards him.

He hadn't been settled under the duvet long when he heard a faint cry. Thinking it was Ruth, he leapt from the sofa-bed, intending to calm her before she could disturb her mother.

As he crossed the hall, he was perturbed to discover it was Jess moaning. As he hesitated, undecided, outside her door, her voice rose to a thin wail, before her screaming sobs rent the air.

Guessing it was a nightmare following the collapse of the wall, he rushed in to try and calm her before she could wake her daughter.

Jess was thrashing about in the bed, making it impossible for his eyes to avoid her nakedness.

Caught unawares by the creamy perfection of her skin, Andrew sat down heavily on the edge of the bed. Then, pulling himself together, he leaned across to pin her shoulders gently to the bed.

Murmuring soothing endearments, he felt the worst of her tremors calm. Relaxing the hold of his right hand, he smoothed back the tortuous tangle of dark hair covering her face.

As the nightmare passed, she slipped back into an untroubled slumber. Thankfully, he tried to replace the bedcovers, but found they were trapped beneath her torso. Intent on carefully extricating them, he was unprepared when she slid both arms round his neck, pulling him to her in an involuntary embrace.

Deeply aware of his body's response to her closeness, but unable to free himself, he whispered her name quietly, hoping to rouse her sufficiently to release her hold.

'Jess,' he repeated, louder this time, only to feel her clutch on him tightening. 'Jess, please let go.' Desperation at the thought of her waking and finding herself in such a compromising situation made him bark the order more harshly than he'd intended.

Immediately she was awake, her confused eyes searching the room before alighting stormily on him.

'You—you—' she gasped, before unclasping her hands and pulling herself as far away from him as she possibly could.

'Jess—' he began, but she was too busy trying to release the duvet from beneath her to listen to anything he had to say.

He leapt from the bed and moved towards the door, only too conscious what she must be thinking.

Grabbing his towelling robe from the chair, he shrugged it on in a belated attempt to hide his arousal.

She glared at him with barely veiled hostility. 'You promised.' A flood of tears accompanied her words.

'Jess, love—'

'Don't call me love…' Her voice was heavy with fear. 'I'm not your love and I never will be. I trusted you…' Here a sob prevented her continuing, but the moment he laid a calming hand on her arm she found her voice again. 'Don't touch me.' She shrank away.

Despairing, he moved to the other side of the room and gave her the facts baldly. 'You had a nightmare. I thought you might wake Ruth with your screaming. My intention was merely to release you from the nightmare.' He considered telling her she had made the advance, but guessed in her present state she wouldn't listen. 'I'm tired,' he concluded icily, 'so if there's nothing you want, I'll try and get some sleep.'

Tearfully she shook her head, and watched wide-eyed as he left the room.

The moment he was gone, Jess allowed her emotions full rein. Silent tears soaked her pillow as she tried to blot out the memory of his treachery. She hadn't been looking for further complications in her life, but when she'd met Andrew they had come uninvited as she had sensed an immediate awareness between them.

But it was not enough. If she was even to consider abandoning her self-imposed celibacy, she needed to be able to trust the man she did it for. Andrew had just proved she couldn't.

The remainder of the night passed with fitful dreams of his many kindnesses intermingling with her dread of losing control of her emotions and the effect it would have on Ruth.

She awoke with the most awful hangover she'd ever experienced—and all on one glass of wine! Wanting to go to the bathroom, she searched for the robe she had borrowed the night before. Suddenly recalling Andrew slinging it over his shoulders, she swore softly and quickly dressed.

'Good morning, Jess.' Andrew's voice startled her, coming from the depths of the armchair when she'd thought he was asleep. 'Sorry about the dressing gown. I would have returned it earlier, but wasn't sure of my reception.'

He grinned wickedly.

Irritated by his flippant attitude, Jess nodded brusquely and, slamming the door behind her, ensconced herself in the bathroom.

As she showered, she asked herself repeatedly how she was ever going to settle back into the safety of her uncomplicated existence with Gwen and Les after this ridiculous escapade.

Despite her attempt to wash her troubles away, she emerged from the bathroom with no clearer an answer than when she had woken. Peeping in to the other room, she found Ruth's bed empty.

The smell of warm baking and freshly brewed coffee drew her towards the kitchen, where she discovered Ruth enjoying an incredibly flaky croissant, liberally coated with jam.

'Hello, Mummy,' she greeted with her mouth full. 'There's one for you. They're scrummy.'

Unwilling to upset the little girl, Jess smiled warily as she joined her daughter in the kitchen.

'That's better. Take a seat and have a croissant before your daughter makes herself sick. Coffee all right?'

Bemused by Andrew's display of domesticity, she nodded. 'A cup of coffee would be very welcome.' She seated herself beside Ruth and kissed the little girl on the cheek.

'Croissant?' Handing her the coffee, he then replenished the bread basket from the oven.

Jess frowned as she sampled one. 'Did you make these yourself, or have you been out shopping already?'

'All my own work,' he informed her proudly, then, unable to keep his counsel any longer, he laughed conspiratorially. 'Well, not quite all. The supermarket assembled them to the part-baked stage. I just finished them off from frozen.'

'Can I have another, Mummy?'

Conscious of his gaze sliding appreciatively over her, Jess felt herself flush as she asked Ruth, 'How many have you had already?'

'Only two. I think a growing girl could manage another, don't you?' He proffered the plate to Ruth without giving Jess a chance to disagree.

'You too,' he insisted.

'No, thanks, but I must say they're certainly tasty.'

'Too tasty to waste. This one is yours.' He slid the remaining croissant onto her plate. 'You'll need something to sustain you for the long trek ahead.'

Torn between curiosity and annoyance at him ignoring her refusal, she asked suspiciously, 'What do you mean? We can get a taxi home.'

'Home? Who mentioned home? We're going to the zoo, aren't we, Ruth?' At her excited nod he added, 'And it's a long walk around the gardens.'

Angered by his assumption that she would agree, Jess countered the suggestion. 'We can't go today. Ruth and I need to get home for a change of clothes.'

Seeing her daughter's stricken face, she added hurriedly. 'We'll go another day, love.'

Ruth burst into tears. 'I want to go today. With Andy.'

Jess compressed her lips. So he'd told the child to call him Andy, had he? Well, she didn't approve and she would put a stop to it. 'I'm sorry, but I've things to catch up on.' Her tone was icy.

He nodded, as if he'd half expected her refusal. 'That's OK,' he informed her jauntily, 'I'll take her and bring her back to you at lunchtime.'

'I'm afraid that won't be possible,' she retaliated stiffly. 'Ruth is coming home with me—now.'

He gave her a long, hard look, then murmured to the little girl, 'I can hear horses. If you look out of your bedroom window, you'll see the riding school on their morning outing.'

Her disappointment temporarily abated, Ruth ran off.

'Whatever you may think of me, why upset Ruth?'

Jess was incensed. 'How dare you accuse me of upsetting her? You shouldn't have made the suggestion without consulting me. I'd already made plans to take her to the zoo for her birthday treat.'

He shrugged. 'Jess, she needs—'

'I'm not interested in what you think she needs. I can assure you there was no problem until you started interfering. Please leave us alone to get on with our lives as we always have.' Her eyes blazing with fury, she pushed back her chair from the table and stormed out of the kitchen.

Tears stinging her eyes, she shut herself in the bathroom. This was even worse than she had imagined in her worst nightmare. She was so attracted to him that she needed all her resolve not to let him take over her life. But she must. He'd proved last night that she couldn't trust him, and the closer she allowed him to get to Ruth, the more traumatic the break, when it came, was going to be.

She needed to get away immediately, and tomorrow she would see what else the agency had to offer. It would be better if neither she nor Ruth saw him ever again.

Splashing her face with cold water, she dabbed her eyes lightly and emerged to find him drawing pictures for Ruth.

With their two heads close over the sheet of paper, they looked as if they belonged together. So much so that she felt a stab of pain at the thought of what she was about to do to her daughter.

'Have you Ruth's inhaler?' he asked quietly. 'I think she might need it.'

'It was in the car. I've another one at home, though. Could I use your phone to ring for a taxi?'

'There's no need to go that far. I'll run you home.' At least he seemed to have accepted that the trip to the zoo was off, but Jess winced at the coldness in his voice.

As he pulled up in Luccombe Gardens, he murmured, 'We need to talk, Jess. Alone.'

'There's nothing left to be said. I think it'll be better if I don't return to the college either. I apologise for letting you down at such short notice.' A sudden thought struck her and she couldn't help the ghost of a grin flitting across her lips. 'And do please tell Lucy it's not because I'm an agency nurse.'

CHAPTER TEN

'CAN'T we go to the zoo, Mummy?' Ruth's plaintive voice from the back seat increased Jess's resolve. Her wheeze was as loud as Jess ever remembered it. The sooner she got the inhaler, and got Andrew out of their lives, the better.

'Not today, love. We must let Andrew get away now.'

'How are you going to manage without transport?'

Jess had been so immersed in her own thoughts that her lack of wheels hadn't occurred to her. 'I—I don't know. I'll work something out.'

'It's the college's responsibility to replace your car. Until we can sort that out, why don't you stay? I could take you to work and bring you home.' He made the offer quietly, watching her face while he did so.

Jess realised she was trapped. Many of the jobs the agency offered were inaccessible without her own car. She wasn't prepared to ask Gwen and Les for any more help than they were already giving. And the college would probably process her claim much quicker if she was on the spot. What else could she do? If she wasn't to lose out on a regular pay packet, she had to accept his offer, much as she didn't want to.

'I guess I'll have to agree.'

Andrew ignored her ungraciousness. 'Great. And by the way, if you're worried about your keys, Sylvia rescued them last night. I rang her.' He looked more cheerful than he had since they'd left the flat. 'Eight forty-five be all right tomorrow?'

Jess nodded. 'But you can pick me up at the school. It's nearer.' She gave him the address, then, taking Ruth's hand, helped her from the car.

'And thank you for all you've done for us. We do appreciate it.'

He raised a disbelieving eyebrow. 'You do? I don't really think so. Otherwise you'd indulge my wish to take Ruth to the zoo. I've wanted to visit it for years and never had anyone to go with. I thought my opportunity had arrived at last.' He assumed an air of deep disappointment.

Jess sighed deeply at the guilt he was arousing within her. He certainly knew how to attack her conscience. All the while she'd believed he was doing it for Ruth, it had been easy. Now he was expressing his own disappointment, she found it impossible. He might not be trustworthy, but she was too attracted to him physically not to feel a sense of shame at depriving him of the outing. Especially after all he'd done for them, *and* his offer of transport.

'Perhaps another time. I think we both need a quiet day today, after yesterday's excitement.'

She could see he looked suitably disappointed, but, smiling towards Ruth, he pretended to accept her rebuffal stoically. 'If that's what you think's best, we'll have to fall in with it—won't we, Ruth?'

Not really understanding, the little girl wheezed noisily as she watched Andrew climb behind the wheel of the Granada and roar away.

'I like him a lot, Mummy. Don't you?'

Jess nodded. 'He's a good doctor, which keeps him very busy. So we mustn't expect to see him often.'

Ruth's face fell. 'But we can go to the zoo with him soon, can't we?'

Jess knew that now the idea was in her head she wouldn't want to wait for her birthday.

Gwen opened the door to them and, seeing no sign of Andrew, asked, 'Didn't you invite him in?'

Jess shook her head. 'I don't want to encourage him.'

'Encourage him? Where's your manners?' Hands on her hips, Gwen was obviously annoyed. 'After the care he's taken of you? Isn't that rather rude?'

'Andy was going to take me to the zoo, but Mummy wouldn't let him,' Ruth informed Gwen dolefully as, breathing noisily, the little girl led them through to the back of the house.

Gwen looked at Jess with amazement. 'Why ever not? The little one would have enjoyed that. She doesn't often get a chance to escape without one of us in tow.'

'Don't you start criticising the way I'm rearing her as well,' Jess hissed angrily. 'I've had quite enough of that already.'

Gwen didn't answer until Jess had found Ruth's spare inhaler and helped her to use it.

'You'll find Grandpa Les in the back garden,' Gwen told the little girl, who immediately went skipping off to find him.

'Now,' she ordered Jess firmly, 'sit down and tell me what this is all about.'

Jess looked down at her hands, resting in her lap. 'He believes I'm making a bad job of bringing up Ruth. Goodness knows why, but he seems to feel an obligation to do something about it.'

Gwen frowned, 'Why ever would he want to do a thing like that? You've got it all wrong, I'm sure. He's trying to make things easier for you, that's all. And it's about time you swallowed your pride and accepted.' Gwen had never spoken to her so sharply before, and Jess guessed she must be disappointed to discover no flourishing romance.

Upset that no one seemed to understand, Jess shrugged. 'If you must know, he's not to be trusted. I thought I could last night, but I was wrong. I woke—' Jess stopped abruptly, overcome with emotion at the unexpectedly erotic memory of his body close to hers.

'You woke?' Gwen prompted.

Suddenly unwilling to confide her innermost fears, Jess finished breathlessly, 'I woke to find he'd broken his promise. I'd rather remain as I am than become involved with a man I can't trust. And he's not good for Ruth either. I can't remember Ruth's asthma ever being so bad. The less we both see of him the better.'

'I don't suppose refusing to let him take her to the zoo helped!'

'Maybe not, but he shouldn't have suggested it without asking me first.'

Gwen shook her head. 'Jess. You are a very attractive woman. Neither Les nor I expect you to shut yourself away for the remainder of your life just because our son is dead. Sure, we'd miss you both, but you've given us enormous pleasure already—and, you know, we aren't getting any younger. We'd never throw you out, but if you did meet someone who cared enough, it would make us very happy.'

Jess crossed to Gwen and gave her a hug. 'I know that, but Andrew Brent is not that person.'

As Gwen gave a snort of disbelief and muttered, 'We'll see,' Jess made her way up to her room and hesitantly surveyed herself in the mirror, before slowly changing out of the clothes that had become so grubby during the rescue the day before.

She watched Ruth running happily up and down the garden path behind Les. She was much better already, and Jess didn't put that all down to the inhaler. She guessed it was partly due to her being away from the tense atmosphere between herself and Andrew.

She threw herself onto the bed in a frenzy of despair. Other one-parent families coped. What was she doing wrong? It would be all too easy to drift into a relationship with Andrew, but if it didn't work out, surely that would damage her daughter more than if she remained on her own until Ruth was older?

No, she had definitely made the right decision. She must learn to ignore her feelings for Andrew and do what she thought was best for the child.

Resolutely she climbed from the bed, and, looking out some clean clothes for Ruth, called the girl up to the bedroom.

'When we've cleaned you up, we'll go and help Granny with the vegetables, shall we?'

Ruth nodded. 'Then can we go to the zoo? Please, Mummy.'

'Wouldn't you rather take a friend on your birthday?'

'That's weeks away.'

'We'll have to see if we can manage something sooner, then.'

Ruth looked partly mollified, and ran ahead of her to see if Gwen needed any help.

When the little girl was eventually out of earshot, Jess confided hesitantly, 'You were right, Gwen. I shouldn't make Ruth's life a misery because *I* have a problem with Andrew, so I think I'll take her to the zoo after all. If we could perhaps have an early lunch?'

'No problem. You'll ring Andrew, then, will you?'

'No. Apart from work, I think the less we see of him, the better. Ruth will soon forget him then.'

Gwen pursed her lips with disapproval, but didn't argue, and when, over lunch, Les heard what was proposed, he offered to drive them all to the zoo. 'It's a long time since Granny and I visited the animals.'

'The zoo? Today? Goody, goody.' Ruth bounced up and down on her chair excitedly. 'With Andy?'

Jess shook her head. 'Not today, but that shouldn't stop us having a good time.'

Torn between the thrill of a trip to the zoo and the sad news that Andrew wouldn't be with them, Ruth's lower lip began to wobble. 'Is that because he's busy again?'

Jess nodded, and, trying to ignore the small voice of conscience that told her she was only doing this to prevent Ruth going with Andrew at a later date, she accepted Les's offer with a smile.

By two o'clock they were outside the main entrance. A small queue had formed, so while Les parked the car Jess offered to get the tickets.

While Jess queued, Gwen took Ruth's hand and walked

towards the gate to point out the photographs of animals displayed. A moment later Ruth came rushing back excitedly.

'Mummy! Andy's got our tickets. Come on, he's waiting for us.' Taking her mother's hand, she dragged her up to the front of the queue.

Gwen was already chatting nonchalantly to Andrew, and included Jess in the conversation. 'Wasn't that a stroke of luck? We arrived just in time. It was nearly Andrew's turn to buy his ticket when Ruth spotted him. I was just explaining about Les parking the car.'

Unable to believe it could be a coincidence, Jess pursed her lips angrily and muttered, 'Very convenient.' She held out her hand containing the admission money. 'I think you should find that right, Dr Brent.'

His eyes widened in amused amazement at her formality, but he responded in the same vein. 'That's quite all right, Nurse Fenn. My treat.'

Jess inhaled deeply before snapping angrily, 'We don't need your charity.'

He grinned. 'Oh, it's not. It's payment for the packed lunches you supply me with.'

Impatient to get on with the tour of the zoo, Ruth pointed excitedly to Les coming along the road. 'Grandpa's here. We can go in now.'

Recognising she could do nothing else, Jess replaced the money in her purse as she followed them in through the entrance.

'Can we see the penguins first. Please?' Ruth was hopping excitedly from one foot to the other and squealed with delight as Gwen and Les said they would take her to watch them feeding.

Jess tried to catch up with them, but Andrew took her arm and pulled her back. 'In a minute. I want to see them, too. But first I want you to promise you won't spoil this for Ruth.'

Jess glared at him. 'You are always accusing me of spoiling things. You're the one gate-crashing our outing.'

Andrew shook his head. 'It was you who said you had things to catch up on today. How could I know you would change your mind?' He grinned impishly.

'Did Gwen ring you?' Jess asked suspiciously.

Andrew looked at her with narrowed eyes. 'You're becoming paranoid, Jess. I told you I wanted to see round the zoo. I came alone because I guessed you'd never let Ruth out of your sight long enough for her to come with me.' When she didn't answer, he grasped her arm and swung her round to face him. 'You wouldn't, would you?'

'I intended to when I said it.'

'But you had second thoughts?'

'No—not—'

'Then what are you doing here today?'

Unable to truthfully sustain her denial, Jess dropped her gaze to the floor. 'Ruth was upset. I felt guilty.'

'Not guilty enough, though, to let *me* know you'd changed your mind.' Contemptuously he thrust her arm from his hold and ran over to join Ruth by the penguins. When the surging crowd prevented her seeing the keeper throwing the fish, he hoisted the little girl onto his shoulders to give her a better view.

Throughout the remainder of the afternoon he chattered animatedly to Ruth and her grandparents, but rarely spoke to Jess. And when he did, his tone was icy.

Though she knew she deserved it, Jess was hurt by him behaving as if he was blameless. So she was dismayed to hear Gwen's invitation as they made their way out of the zoo at closing time. 'If you've nothing to get back for, why don't you join us for a meal this evening, Andrew?'

'That's very kind of you, Gwen, but I think not. Another day perhaps.' He looked towards Jess as he spoke, but she ignored him.

He walked them back to their car, then, taking his leave,

reminded Jess, 'I'll see you at the school. Quarter to nine, wasn't it?'

She nodded numbly and slid into the back of Les's Metro beside her daughter.

Apart from Ruth's excited chatter about the animals, little was said throughout the meal that Jess prepared.

However, the moment Ruth was settled in bed, the dam of Gwen's disapproval broke. 'What's the matter with you, behaving that way? That poor doctor nearly out of his mind with love for you and you can't speak a civil word to him. You didn't even thank him for buying your entrance ticket.'

'It's not me he loves.' More upset than she was prepared to admit at Andrew's behaviour towards her, Jess shut her eyes to prevent the tears spilling out. The unfairness of it. He'd hardly addressed a word to her all afternoon and now she was being blamed.

'Leave it, love.' Les Halton placed an arm affectionately round his wife's waist. 'It's their affair after all.'

Gwen sniffed. 'I only wish it was.'

Jess rose from her chair and fled up the stairs, and locked the bedroom door behind her. If it was only herself, trust him or not, she would throw caution to the wind where Andrew was concerned. But she couldn't risk Ruth's happiness. She must be sensible and ignore the dictates of her heart until Ruth no longer needed her.

Jess and Ruth arrived at the school gates on Monday morning to find Andrew waiting in his car. As he clambered out, Ruth ran towards him, squealing with delight.

'Andy! Have you come to see my school?'

He ruffled her hair affectionately. 'I've been watching all your friends arrive. I think you ought to join them inside. I must get Mummy to work as she has no car.'

Ruth nodded sagely. 'We'll have one again soon, won't we?'

'You know I told you we wouldn't have a car for a couple of weeks at least,' Jess admonished her crossly. 'Now get on inside or you'll make Dr Brent late for work.'

Startled by her mother's tone, Ruth pecked her hastily on the cheek and scampered through the school gates.

Andrew turned to Jess with raised eyebrows. 'That was a bit hard on her, wasn't it?' Without waiting for a reply, he opened the passenger door and gestured impatiently for her to climb in.

Aware of a guilty flush staining her cheeks, Jess was thankful he couldn't see her face. She hadn't intended to speak so sharply, but Ruth's pleasure every time she set eyes on Andrew brought out the worst in her.

He slammed the driver's door and they roared towards the college in an uncomfortable silence.

A stealthy glance at his profile revealed not the anger Jess had expected, but an air of hopeless resignation that hurt her more than his wrath would ever have done.

As he parked his car, her mind was made up. There was no way she could go on working with him. Even now she was finding it difficult to resist the urge to take him in her arms and tell him she loved him, but a relationship needed to be based on more than physical responses. For Ruth's sake, if not her own.

He helped her out of the car, his touch burning a possessive brand onto her skin. Irritably she pulled her arm free. 'Thanks for the lift, Andrew.'

'Are you sure you feel fit for work?'

She gave him a straight look. 'Perfectly, thanks. The scratches are healing fast and the bruises will soon be gone.' Which is more than I can say for the psychological ones, she thought.

As they approached the surgery entrance, she told him, 'Andrew, I'll stay only until the weekend. I won't be accepting the permanent position after all. You should be able to find someone else by then, and I should have found some means of transport.'

Ignoring the look of disbelief on his face, she pushed open the door into the waiting room and called brightly, 'Good morning, Lucy. Everything all right?'

Andrew crossed to his own room in silence, while Jess made her way into the treatment room to start her day's work.

Lucy followed her in. 'How was your weekend? Quiet?'

Jess smiled ruefully. 'That was the last thing you could call it.'

'What happened?'

'It's a long story. Part of the burnt-out building at the Roundings collapsed. I happened to be there. I have scratches to prove it,' she joked.

Her eyes wide, Lucy pressed for details.

'I'll tell you later. How was your weekend?'

Lucy smiled. 'Fantastic. Grant and I went walking in the Cotswolds yesterday. Oh, Jess, I'm so thankful the porter made that mistake with my note, otherwise we might never have met.'

Mention of the note reinforced Jess's decision. Andrew hadn't entirely believed her about that either.

To her surprise, the morning sped by, but when she had to check with Andrew about the medication for a student with asthma, Jess held her breath in case he turned the conversation to Ruth's asthma, or even tried to persuade her to change her mind. Paradoxically, she was disappointed when he didn't.

As lunchtime approached Lucy asked if she would like to assist with the surgery at the Roundings site.

'If you don't mind I'd rather stay here for the afternoon, but I would like to pop down to the shops at lunchtime. I'm lost without my car.'

'Where is it?'

Lucy listened in amazement as Jess told her of the events of Saturday afternoon. She carefully withheld any details of Saturday night.

'Your little girl must have been terrified. Is she all right?'

'Fine.' Jess laughed. 'Apart from an asthma attack. And that soon settled when I could get to her spare inhaler. Children are surprisingly resilient.'

They didn't get a further opportunity to gossip, for no sooner had Jess returned from the shops than it was time for Andrew to leave with Lucy.

'I'll see you later.'

Jess tried to ignore the disturbing tone of his voice and settled down to her afternoon's work, which included another long and useful chat with Melissa, the married mother-to-be student.

Nevertheless, as five o'clock approached, she became increasingly apprehensive about the journey home.

But Andrew didn't mention her decision.

Instead, he told her what he'd learned at Roundings that afternoon. 'Sylvia had all the news. It *was* the students Zoe complained about that caused the building to collapse. Silly fools, trespassing like that.'

'What'll happen to them?'

'They've gone already. Good job too.'

He parked the car in Luccombe Gardens and all her fears returned as he turned to her with a surprising suggestion.

'Before you go, we need to talk. I'd like you to tell me about Larry.'

Jess stiffened. 'It's not something I want to discuss.'

'Jess, love. I'm worried about you. I think you're carrying around an unnecessarily large burden of guilt. That's why my accusations about Larry hit you so hard. They were too near what you believe yourself, weren't they?'

'Are you psychoanalysing me now?' She glared at him angrily.

'Not exactly, but it's my guess you walked out on him when he decided to go to Bangladesh.'

Jess gasped. 'You've got it all wrong. It was Larry's idea I stayed with my parents while he was away.'

Andrew shook his head. 'Because you didn't want him to go?'

'Get out of my life, Andrew. Everything was running smoothly until I came to work with you. I just want to return to that tranquillity. I was happy then.'

'Happy? I don't think so somehow. I think you're mistaking loneliness for tranquillity.'

'Maybe. But while I have Ruth to consider that's the way it's got to be.'

'It doesn't have to be, Jess.'

'Well, it's going to be,' she told him firmly, opening the car door and climbing out. 'Thank you for bringing me home. I'll find my own way in tomorrow.'

He shrugged and gave her a maddening grin. 'I'll be outside the school at the same time.'

Jess was tempted to send Ruth to school with Gwen the next day, but in the end she decided that was going too far. And she needn't have worried either. Andrew talked about nothing but work.

'Ian's having his first dialysis today.'

'Poor lad. Do they know what caused the failure?'

'Pyelonephritis—he must have had waterworks infections as a young child that left the kidney scarred.'

'Ouch, nasty. How long will the dialysis have to go on?'

'Until a suitable kidney is found for transplantation. That's the difficulty. There is such a shortage it could be a long wait. It's going to be disruptive to his studies.'

He broke the ensuing silence with news of another patient. 'I saw Mary last night. No complications, so she should be home by the end of the week. Our prompt action prevented *her* going on to kidney failure.'

'Mary?' Jess frowned. 'How?'

'When crushed tissues are released, they swell as fluid pours out from the blood, and the injured muscles produce toxins which can be absorbed into the bloodstream and cause renal failure.'

'I didn't realise it could be quite so serious. Thank goodness we were there.' She didn't enlarge on the subject in case it brought the conversation back to *her* injuries.

Andrew sighed, unmistakably put out by her refusal to open up.

The remainder of the week followed a similar pattern, but Jess rebuffed his every attempt to draw her to chat about anything other than work.

She accepted gratefully, however, when he offered to help her fill in the mounds of paperwork applying for compensation for her car. But, as the finance officer had warned them it wouldn't appear overnight, she wasn't surprised when the end of the week arrived without any news.

Jess was relieved when Lucy went with Andrew to the Roundings site on Friday. And not only because of Andrew. Her memories of the previous Saturday were still too vivid for her to want to visit the site yet. She supposed he'd realised that and was being considerate again!

When Andrew dropped her at Luccombe Gardens that evening, he murmured politely, 'Thank you for all you've done for us at the college. If I can help in any way, Jess, please let me know. And I promise I'll keep chasing up the car.'

He made no attempt to persuade her to change her mind about the job, merely wished her good luck.

Perched on the windowsill, Ruth banged the window in an attempt to gain his attention, but Andrew ignored her and drove off.

Ruth's disappointment was keenly shared by Jess, for despite her protestations a small part of her deep within had hoped he might care enough to try and persuade her to stay.

Her life could never revert to what it had been. Her feelings were too deeply disturbed for that. But after Larry's death she had made up her mind that the next time she gave herself to a man she would be married. And, however much of a fancy Andrew had taken to Ruth, that was not a reason to do so. Not that he'd asked. He probably just wanted another live-in affair—this time complete with ready-made family.

Swallowing hard against the lump in her throat, Jess

made her way into the house and immersed herself in the evening routine.

While Ruth played in the bath, and Gwen prepared the evening meal, Jess tentatively explained her decision not to return to the college to Gwen and Les. Expecting Gwen to protest, she was taken aback by their agreeing it was probably all for the best.

'It's your decision, after all. So if you're happy, that's fine by us.' Disinterestedly, Gwen began to set the table.

Jess no longer thought she *was* happy with her decision. She was already bereft at the thought of not seeing Andrew again, and she still had no car of her own. As long as everyone had wanted her to keep the job, she'd been determined to oppose them. Now no one seemed to care, she was beginning to regret her stance. But she had too much pride to say so.

After a week of struggling with public transport to and from work that entailed unsocial hours, Jess decided to take a few days off and take Ruth to visit her other grandmother.

As Gwen saw her off on the train, she asked, 'Will you be back in time for Ruth's birthday?'

Jess nodded. 'She wants to share her birthday tea with you and Les. I'll probably see you Wednesday, but I won't work Thursday and Friday so that I can get everything ready.'

Andrew was overworked. The nurse the agency sent as Jess's replacement was exactly as Lucy had described agency nurses to be. He knew by Monday mid-morning she wouldn't last, and was not at all surprised when she didn't reappear on Tuesday. Her replacement wasn't much better. She lasted three days.

After a hectic morning surgery the following Monday, he found himself missing his shared lunch with Jess more than ever. That wasn't all he missed. He'd lost his heart to

Jess and her daughter and he wanted them back in his life. But how to override her determination to shut him out?

If only he could think of some way to convince her that he was to be trusted and that he trusted her, but nothing he'd said in the past had made any impression on her.

Sighing deeply, he began to sift desultorily through the remaining applications for Joanne's replacement, but he found faults with each one. None of their qualifications matched up to Jess's.

He sighed deeply. It was no good. Somehow he must persuade her to return. She was needed in the surgery and he needed her in his life as well. Even if she would agree to nothing more than a working relationship to start with, it would at least give him a chance to try and change her mind about him personally.

He pushed the papers away and reached for the telephone.

'Hello, Gwen. It's Andrew Brent. Do you know where Jess is working this week?'

'Nice to hear from you, Andrew. Have you news of her car?'

Impatiently he countered the query. 'No. It's early days yet. I just wanted a word with her.'

'They're visiting Jess's mother for a few days.'

'Oh! I see. How long d'you think she'll be away?'

'Jess won't want Ruth away from school too long, and they'll definitely be back for Ruth's seventh birthday on Friday.'

'Ruth's seven? This Friday?' Andrew exclaimed thoughtfully. 'I—I thought she was older… Oh, God, I don't know what I thought,' he added lamely. His heart contracted painfully as he replaced the receiver; he was aware that he had just learnt something momentous.

Leaning back in his chair, he closed his eyes in despair. Only the day before he'd noticed in his diary that the following week he would have been the Student Health Doctor for seven years. That meant it was exactly seven years this week since he had done that locum stint at the isolation hospital. Friday would be seven years to the day since Larry had died.

Pounding his forehead, he knew he'd made the biggest misjudgement of his life when he hadn't pressed Jess to explain. No wonder she'd refused to have anything further to do with him.

The poor girl must have been in labour while Larry was dying, and he had accused her of being heartless. Oh, what a fool he'd been! Why hadn't he tried to find out the facts before blowing his top? He'd known the moment he walked away that he loved her, that whatever she'd done in the past didn't matter. Now he knew she'd done nothing, he should be grovelling at her feet.

Would she ever forgive him? He checked his appointment book for Friday and found the afternoon was so far relatively quiet. He struck a line through the late afternoon part of the page and wrote, 'No appointments please'. His decision made, the next three days dragged interminably, despite the hectic increase in his workload with only Lucy to assist.

The moment four-thirty arrived on Friday, he was ready to leave. 'I'll see you Monday, Lucy.'

Unsure what a seven-year-old girl might want for her birthday, he had purchased a simple computer with the proviso that the shop would take the unopened box back if she already had one.

As he climbed from his car in Luccombe Gardens, the heavens opened, soaking rapidly through his working suit.

The only answer to his knock on the front door was the sound of merriment from within the solidly built detached house.

CHAPTER ELEVEN

SHIVERING uncomfortably, Andrew knocked more forcefully.

The door swung open to reveal a flushed and excited Ruth wearing a purple paper hat that was slipping over her eyes.

'Andy!' she screamed, and flung herself at him, nearly knocking the gift-wrapped parcel from his arms. 'Have you come for my birthday, Andy? I've got a lovely cake. It's a clown.' She tugged at his arm and turned to find her mother standing behind her. 'Mummy, look who's here!'

Jess met Andrew's eyes warily. 'Wh-what do you want.'

Now they were face to face, he didn't know where to begin and he took refuge in the child's present. 'Gwen told me it was Ruth's birthday. I—I thought she might like this.'

Jess appeared annoyed. 'She has everything she needs—'

Andrew held up a staying hand. 'If she already has a computer—'

Ruth let out a yelp of excitement. 'A computer? For me? Can I see it?'

Jess looked angry now. 'I thought I told you to stop butting in on our lives—'

As she spoke Ruth was jumping up and down, saying, 'Let me see. Let me see.'

A look of hopeless resignation crossed Jess's face. 'You'd better give it to her now you've let her know about it.' She spun round on her heel and made her way back along the hall, as if she wanted no further part in the charade.

Andrew followed hesitantly, helping Ruth to carry the parcel that was too big for the girl to manage alone.

They placed it on the dining room floor and Ruth set about opening it.

'Dr Brent. How nice to see you,' Gwen greeted him warmly.

Suspicious of the over-enthusiastic welcome, especially as he had just admitted that it was Gwen who'd told him about the birthday, Jess watched miserably as Gwen added, 'You're soaked. You must be frozen. Would you like something to eat?'

'I'd love a cup of tea.'

Ruth's feverishly excited eyes glanced up at him. 'You can have a piece of my cake. It's scrumptious.'

Jess still appeared uneasy. 'You'd better sit down.'

'Thanks. I—'

'I might not be able to buy Ruth expensive presents, but—'

'Jess, I didn't think about the cost. I just had no idea what else to get her.'

'You didn't need to get her anything,' she muttered crossly.

He sighed. 'I wanted to.'

Ruth raised her eyes from trying to open the box and, sensing all was not well, looked anxiously from one to the other before shrieking, 'Help me, Andy!'

As Gwen brought in a fresh pot of tea, Andrew raised an apologetic eyebrow and settled down on the floor beside Ruth.

When he eventually managed to get the computer from the box, Ruth was jumping up and down and squealing with excitement.

'Let Dr Brent get his tea, Ruth,' Gwen ordered.

Between sips he lifted the computer onto the dining room table and tried to set it up ready for use. But the instruction book wasn't clear and Ruth was impatient.

When it didn't work immediately, she demanded, 'What's the matter with it, Andy? Is it broken?' She hopped from one leg to the other.

Jess answered. 'Don't you think it's too complicated for a seven-year-old?'

'No.' he was becoming annoyed with Jess's negativity. 'Once it's set up, it should be easy. I saw one working in the shop.'

'Huh.' Jess clearly wasn't impressed.

Ruth looked from her mother to Andrew and back again. 'Don't you like it, Mum? I do. And,' she added in little more than a whisper, 'I like Andy for bringing it.'

As if to keep her as far from him as possible, Jess lifted Ruth onto her knee.

Ruth struggled to escape again.

'Stay here a minute and let Dr Brent concentrate.'

Andrew raised a laconic eyebrow at her formality, and, trying to ignore Jess's hostility, worked methodically through the book. But he still couldn't get anything on the screen. Eventually he sighed. 'I'm sorry, Ruth, but I think I'm going to need help with this. I have a friend who'll look at it for me.'

As he started to pack it back into the box, Jess hugged a subdued Ruth. 'Let's get back to your party and your other presents, shall we?'

The little girl's face fell and she sniffed, 'I'd rather have the computer. Is he taking it away because you don't like it?'

Noticing a wheeze developing, Jess suggested, 'Let's go and find your inhaler, shall we?' She led the little girl upstairs and stood by while she inhaled a couple of puffs.

When there didn't appear to be any improvement, Jess guessed all that excited jumping about hadn't helped, and tried to persuade her to go to bed.

'I want to see Andy first,' she wailed, her wheeze becoming even more pronounced.

Jess took her downstairs again where, clearly troubled by her wheezing, Andrew looked up with a frown. 'Inhaler not working?'

Jess shook her head.

'Have you a peak flow meter?'

Again Jess shook her head.

'I'll get one from my bag.' He strode out to the car and was soon back and asking Ruth to blow into the meter. When she eventually understood what he wanted, the reading clearly didn't please him.

'Does she use a spacer with her inhaler?'

Jess couldn't meet his eyes as she admitted, 'It was crushed in the car.'

He sighed. 'Have you a nebuliser?'

'She doesn't have regular attacks so she doesn't need one,' Jess snapped, her irritability compounded by her anxiety about Ruth. 'Because the attacks are mild.'

'Well, this one isn't. I'll get a nebuliser from the college.'

He swung out of the house and roared off in his car as Jess settled Ruth in an upright position on the settee.

Gwen was hovering nervously. 'Is there anything I can do?'

Jess shook her head. 'I don't think so, thanks. You'll be fine with a little rest, won't you, love?'

'Is Andy coming back?' the little girl asked anxiously.

Jess bit back a sigh. 'Yes. He'll be back soon.' Aware that she hadn't been very welcoming, Jess was suddenly grateful that he had been around at this time. Although she couldn't help wondering if the attack would have happened if he hadn't been.

He was soon back with the nebuliser, and within a short time Ruth looked and sounded better, so Gwen brewed a fresh pot of tea for them all and offered to make Andrew a sandwich. He shook his head. 'I was rather hoping to take Jess out to dinner later.' He turned to her. 'Would you agree to that?'

Feeling trapped, Jess looked appealingly towards Gwen, who, deliberately misreading the look, encouraged, 'You go dear. It'll do you good to get out. We'll keep an eye on Ruth.'

Before Jess could answer, the doorbell rang.

'That'll be Sylvia,' Andrew told them as he went to let her in.

Jess felt a familiar lump plummet to the pit of her stomach. She couldn't believe he could be so shameless. He'd just asked her out to dinner and yet he'd known Sylvia was coming to meet him here!

When they came back into the room, he tweaked Ruth on the cheek. 'You remember Sylvia, don't you?'

Ruth nodded.

'I thought we wouldn't wait until tomorrow, so I rang her from the health centre. She's a whizz with computers.'

As they set up the machine again on the dining room table, Jess watched in silence. Within minutes it was working.

'How come it didn't do that for me?' Andy asked.

Sylvia grinned. 'A little bit of expertise goes a long way. It was a loose connection.'

With Ruth seated contentedly beside Sylvia, watching her every move, Jess felt tears springing to her eyes. To hide them, she carried the dirty dishes out to the kitchen.

Andrew followed her. 'Is there anything more I can do, or would you like me to go?'

'She's never had such a bad attack before.'

'You're saying it was my fault for being here?'

Jess looked down at the floor. 'Not exactly. If I hadn't been so angry at you barging in, there'd probably have been no problem.'

He slipped an arm along her shoulder. 'So we're both to blame. Oh, Jess. I've been so foolish.'

Startled, Jess jerked her head up to meet his gaze for the first time. 'You foolish? In—in what way?'

Andrew shrugged. 'In every way.'

He moved his hand to the small of her back and pulled her to him. She tried to pull away from his grasp, but he tightened his hold on her and swung her round to face him again, and kissed her soundly.

'When I saw Larry's photo I guess I felt I'd let you down by not keeping him alive, even though there was nothing more I could have done. That evening I brought the form, I'd hoped to discover if you felt the same way I did. I shouldn't have taken it out on you, though. That was unforgivable. But I could hardly believe it when I realised you were the Jessica who'd written that letter to Larry.

'I think I've loved you since that moment you walked into the surgery and threatened to walk right out again, but I seem destined not to be given a chance to tell you. Please, please believe me, and this time listen to what I'm telling you. Trust me.'

In her exhausted state his use of the word 'trust' caused her pent-up tears to flow. She so wanted to lean on someone. She raised her wet eyes to meet his and whispered, 'I—I think I love you, too, Andrew.'

'I'm sure you do, but I didn't know how to make *you* believe it.' He took both Jess's hands in his own. 'Let me explain something, though, before we get disturbed again.'

'Explain what?' Jess asked warily, suddenly afraid she was about to hear something she didn't want to.

'I know now that I was totally out of order when I berated you for not visiting Larry when he was dying. I've worked out that you must have been in labour about that time, which wouldn't have given you much of a chance.'

'Not a lot,' Jess told him wryly. 'Especially as I'd gone into labour too soon. Larry had told me what date he'd be back on, and he'd expected me to meet him.'

He groaned. 'Ruth was premature? That's why—'

He was prevented from saying more by Jess placing a finger over his lips and then kissing him.

His arms tightened around her until she could barely breathe, but she didn't want the moment to end. When at last he released her, she was sure her knees would no longer support her.

'Can you ever forgive me?'

'There's nothing to forgive.'

He sighed and murmured, 'I wish that was true.'

'It is. Let's forget that evening ever happened.' She smiled, and as he lowered his head she kissed him gently. 'We've both made some stupid mistakes.'

'You're incredible, Jess. Do you know that?' He took her in his arms again and this time her lips gave the response they both wanted.

When at last he released her, he murmured, 'Oh, Jess, I don't deserve you.'

He kissed her wet eyelids gently and murmured soothing endearments against her hair, and the scent of him mingled with his familiar aftershave sent her emotions into overdrive.

Once Ruth knew how to work the computer, Sylvia left quietly and a tired Ruth went to bed quite happily. 'Thank you, Andy.'

She kissed his cheek and he murmured, 'See you tomorrow.'

'Tomorrow? Really?' Ruth looked towards her mother for confirmation.

'I think he'd like you to show him how a computer works,' Jess taunted lightly.

As they walked down the stairs together, he told her, 'Any more cracks like that and I might change my mind about giving you dinner.'

Jess laughed, suddenly feeling much more confident.

It was already late, so Andrew gave Gwen the number of his radio-pager in case Ruth became worse again. 'But I don't expect she will,' he told her confidently.

Despite him taking her to one of the most expensive restaurants in Bradstoke, Jess hardly knew what she was eating. She was too engrossed in all he had to say to her. Until he started to quiz her about Ruth's asthma. Then Jess felt guilty.

'Who's looking after Ruth's asthma?'

'Our GP.'

'Has she seen a consultant?'

'I told you, her asthma has been mild up to now. I just get a repeat prescription when I need it.'

'They don't have an asthma clinic where she's monitored?'

Jess hung her head. 'They do, but I can rarely get there.'

'It's like the cobbler's children who have no shoes. While you're away looking after other asthmatics, your own daughter is neglected.'

Jess tried to defend herself. 'She's not neglected. You can see that for yourself.'

'I'm only teasing. We medics are all the same. We're either hypochondriacal or we ignore everything. But Ruth is not a relative—yet—so I intend to arrange for her to be checked out by the best chest man I know. He's my favourite uncle!'

'Won't he mind?'

'Families do have their uses. I should think young Ian back at the college thinks that, too. His father has two good compatible kidneys and so is donating one to his son.'

'That's fantastic news, Andrew.'

As they walked up the path to the front door, he murmured in her ear, 'It's late, so I won't come in, but I'll collect you at two tomorrow.'

'What for?'

'Some time to ourselves.'

'But my Saturdays are for Ruth—'

'Ah-ah-ah,' he cautioned. 'You can leave her for once. Sylvia will be there. She's promised to teach Ruth more about the computer.'

'Sylvia?' Jess queried in horror. 'But—'

'But nothing. It'll do her good. Sylvia knows all about computers. More than I do.' He grinned. 'She's even beginning to realise children are human beings after all.'

Fear gripped Jess again and she felt herself tense. 'So—so you—you—and Sylvia—'

He kissed her long and hard. 'Might get together again? No. She doesn't want children of her own, and anyway, that wasn't the only difference between us. I can assure you that that relationship is well and truly over and done with.'

When he finally released Jess from his arms, she was sure she was already dreaming. But she didn't want to wake from it and so was soon in bed.

It was still pouring with rain when he collected her on Saturday afternoon. 'What can we do in this weather?' she asked as she opened the door to him.

He whispered, 'I'm taking you back to my place for some unfinished business.'

'You're wicked,' she told him, as with a grin he went through to see Ruth.

'Hi,' she greeted him abstractedly, but Jess could see Ruth had no interest in either herself or Andy while Sylvia was teaching her all she could about the computer.

She realised just how foolish she had been to get uptight at Ruth enjoying Andrew's company so much. Children were fickle with their affections.

The moment they were inside the flat door, Andrew took her in his arms and started to remove her wet outer garment. 'And don't think I'm going to stop here,' he told her as he slipped her jumper over her head and carried her through to his bedroom. 'I think you need me as much as I need you.'

'Oh, Andrew. I knew that first Monday I walked into the health centre that I was attracted to you, but I tried to ignore how I felt. I thought you were probably married.'

'Me, married?' He laughed. 'Whatever gave you that idea?'

'Your apparent understanding of the havoc children can create in a well-ordered routine.'

He looked surprised. 'Really? I'm amazed I gave that impression.'

Embarrassed, she couldn't meet his eyes. 'Perhaps you didn't exactly. I think it was probably because I was sub-consciously searching for someone like Larry and—'

'I know, love. I know. That's why I'm here and why

you're here with me. I love you so much, Jess. I'm going to marry you. With Ruth as chief bridesmaid.'

'Married?' she echoed. 'Oh, Andrew. Do you really mean it? Ruth would love that.'

'Of course I mean it. I love you, and want you with me always so that I can look after you in the way you deserve.'

She happily succumbed to his caresses for a long moment before saying hesitantly, 'I don't know that I'm as deserving as you imagine. Let's face it, this whole mix-up has been my own fault, Andrew. If I'd explained about Larry in the beginning, the problem would never have arisen.'

She raised her eyes apologetically before continuing, 'Perhaps I *was* too satisfied with my own little world for my own good. Or Ruth's, for that matter. But I want to make up for it now, love.'

Andrew placed his forefinger over her lips.

'I don't need to know anything more to love you, or to trust you.' His kiss, long and deep, reinforced his words, and a quivering excitement rippled through her body. She pushed him away playfully. 'I wish I'd trusted you half as much. I thought at first you were criticising my bringing up of Ruth.'

'So that's what upset you at Roundings, was it? Did Sylvia have something to do with that by any chance?' he asked suspiciously.

Jess laughed. 'Not exactly, but she did make me think it was Ruth you were interested in and not me.'

He gasped. 'My only intention was to prevent you being unhappy when she eventually makes her own way in life.'

'I know, but I think by that time I wanted to believe the worst of you, and then you gave me the perfect opportunity when you came into my bedroom after promising—'

'Don't you dare say that,' Andrew threatened playfully. 'I came to comfort you in your nightmare and you threw yourself naked at me. Honestly, I've never been so surprised in my life, and as I frantically tried to escape your hold you woke up and accused me! I couldn't believe it.' With a stifled groan he took her in his arms as just the memory of that night aroused him beyond control.

But this time Jess knew it was time to forget the hold the past had had on her and allow her own emotions a free rein. She reached out and slowly started to undress him as he had done her. 'My turn to see you naked,' she whispered as they sank onto the bed together.

Later, as they lay quietly in one another's arms, she said seriously, 'I loved Larry, Andrew. Loved him dearly. As I told you, his parents were against him marrying as a student so we lived together without them knowing. When he went off to Bangladesh and I was pregnant, I admit I was furious—I felt he was letting me down. So he packed me off home so Mum could take care of me. If he couldn't get what he wanted one way, there was always another solution. Nothing ever fazed him. Mum liked him, so did my dad.

'When I went into labour we tried and tried to contact him. We could get no reply from Les and Gwen either. Of course I found out later they were by his bedside.'

Andrew nodded. 'One thing we couldn't understand was his lack of immunity to hepatitis. Why wasn't he vaccinated?'

'He refused to risk a third injection because he'd had a reaction to the first two doses—the second worse than the first. As his trip was unofficial, no one checked. I begged him to get another opinion, but he could be very stubborn at times. But I loved him. And he loved me.'

Pent-up tears cascaded down her cheeks as she described him to Andrew. 'He was so looking forward to our baby, but it made him all the more determined to use his two weeks' holiday to do what he could do for refugee babies in Bangladesh.'

'We had a dreadful row, and then his flight was brought forward so I didn't have a chance to say goodbye, and I never knew if any of my letters reached him.'

'I can assure you at least one did. That was where we got your parents' address,' he told her quietly, while rubbing the nape of her neck gently with his hand.

'And they were at the maternity hospital trying frantically to locate Larry.'

Tears sprang to her eyes as she recalled the vivid memories. 'The first I knew at the time was when Mum saw it in the paper. I couldn't believe it. They'd just delivered Ruth and I needed him.' She sobbed brokenly, before rousing herself to explain, 'I couldn't get to the funeral because I was so weak and Ruth was in the SCBU. I sent flowers, though. Red roses.'

Andrew nodded thoughtfully. 'I remember—but no signature. Why?'

She shrugged. 'If Gwen and Les had realised at that stage we'd been living together they'd have been devastated. I thought they had enough to cope with without that.'

'You thought of others before yourself even then?' Andrew shook his head in amazement. 'How did they find out about Ruth?'

'My mother persuaded me I ought to contact them. Mum knew, and by that time I think I'd come to realise, exactly how they must feel having lost their only child. I wanted them to have the chance to know their grandchild.'

'So you all lived happily ever after?'

'Not immediately. Things were very fraught at first, especially when they realised how Larry had deceived them.

'When Dad had to retire through ill health, I knew I had to get a job. I decided I'd be better off where I was known, and that Dad would have peace and quiet if we moved out.' She snuggled closer to Andrew's body in an attempt to shut out the unpleasant memories.

'I decided I owed it to Gwen and Les to let them know I'd be in the area. They were already regretting their behaviour, and offered me a home. They are darlings, really. I can well understand how distressed they must have been at the time. My only regret is that my father died not long afterwards, but as Mum decided to return to work she couldn't have done what Gwen and Les do for me.' She smiled wanly. 'You know the rest.'

'Maybe, but thank you for telling me, love. Larry's death has always stuck in my mind because I was doing a locum job, and because he was someone from our own profession whom we thought was on the mend. We couldn't believe it when he relapsed so unexpectedly. He'd become ill on the flight and that was why he was rushed to the nearest isolation hospital the moment they landed.'

'Oh, Andrew.' Jess's cry was anguished. 'I think I'll love you all the more because we both cared so much about Larry.'

'We need never talk about this again unless you want to, but I think it's important that Larry isn't forgotten. For your sake and for Ruth's.' He ran a featherlight finger the length of her spine before adding, 'And I want to make it clear here and now. Ruth is your daughter. You bring her up the way you think best. She's a delightful, well-balanced girl who does you credit. All I ever wanted to do was to make a life for you outside that of being Ruth's mother. *And* I wanted you both to be financially secure. When we marry, I'll achieve both.'

Jess squirmed in delight as his caresses became increasingly intimate. 'I *do* love you, Andrew Brent.' Suddenly serious, she pushed herself away from contact with him. 'There's just one question I want to know the answer to.'

'Ye-es?'

'Have you and Gwen kept in touch since that day at the zoo?'

He grinned and encircled her with his arms. 'That's one answer you don't deserve to know. But I'll put you out of your misery. She didn't tell me you were going to the zoo that Sunday; I just knew you'd take Ruth to prevent me doing so later. And the only time I've spoken to Gwen since was when I rang to ask where you were working, and she told me you were away but would be back for Ruth's birthday.' He kissed her on the forehead, then the nose, and finally the lips. 'Satisfied?'

'With the answer or your kisses?' she teased.

'Both. Hey, I've just had an idea. If we marry sooner rather than later you could give up work and look after Ruth—and perhaps think about helping Mel out with her baby. It would only be a short-term commitment and you said you'd like to do it.'

'It's tempting, but it would leave you without a second nurse again.'

'I know,' he pondered thoughtfully, 'that's my only worry. But with time on our side, we'll find the right person. And I'm sure Lucy will benefit from your expertise in the meantime.'

'You are? When we never get a moment to work together?'

'You will. We heard last week that our secretary-cum-receptionist will be back from sick leave on Monday, freeing you both from much of the administrative burden.

'And Lucy's pretty good already. She's worked wonders since your defection, especially with Mike—you remember, the lad with glandular fever. He's had a really nasty dose and she's visited every day, sometimes twice *and* in her own time. He's really appreciated her support.'

'I'm glad you've realised her potential at last!'

'Ganging up on me already, are you? I always did, until *you* came along to dazzle me with your presence,' he teased.

'So what if you find an even better replacement?' she asked with a pout.

He kissed her gently. 'Believe me, there is no one who can match your qualities. And not only as a treatment room nurse.' He hugged her tightly to him. 'You are the only one for me. Just remember that.'

MILLS & BOON®

Medical Romance™

COMING NEXT MONTH

HERO'S LEGACY by Margaret Barker

Jackie had never expected to feel like this again and it was great! She realised that she'd been living in the past and now Tom was going to help her face the future.

FORSAKING ALL OTHERS by Laura MacDonald

Book 3 of the Matchmaker quartet

Siobhan thought that David was gorgeous but a playboy. If he wanted her he'd have to prove he was serious—it was marriage or nothing!

TAKE ONE BACHELOR by Jennifer Taylor

Could this gorgeous woman really be his new assistant? But Matthew wasn't tempted, after all he'd just decided to steer clear of women, hadn't he?

A MATTER OF PRACTICE by Helen Shelton

Kids and Kisses...another heart-warming story

The birth of their son and their heavy work-load had put a lot of strain on Claire and Ben's marriage. Ben was sure they could work it out but could he convince Claire?

On sale from 13th July 1998

Available at most branches of WH Smith, John Menzies, Martins, Tesco, Volume One and Safeway

MILLS & BOON®

The perfect summer read for those long, hot, lazy days...

Summer Loving

Have fun in the sun with this fabulous bumper collection of four light-hearted, sexy novels—

It Happened One Week by JoAnn Ross

Male For Sale by Tiffany White

Traci On The Spot by Marie Ferrarella

First Date Honeymoon by Diane Pershing

Brought to you at the special price of just £4.99

On sale from 18th May 1998

Available from WH Smith, Tesco, Asda, John Menzies, Martins, Volume One and all good paperback stockists

MILLS & BOON®

Elizabeth Gage

The Collection

A compelling read of three full-length novels by
best-selling author of A Glimpse of Stocking

Intimate

Number One

A Stranger to Love

"...Gage is a writer of style and intelligence..."
—Chicago Tribune

On sale from 13th July 1998   Price £5.25

Available at most branches of WH Smith, John Menzies,
Martins, Tesco, Asda, and Volume One

SPOT THE DIFFERENCE

Spot all ten differences between the two pictures featured below and you could win a year's supply of Mills & Boon® books—FREE! When you're finished, simply complete the coupon overleaf and send it to us by 31st December 1998. The first five correct entries will each win a year's subscription to the Mills & Boon series of their choice. What could be easier?

F8C

Please turn over for details of how to enter ⇨

HOW TO ENTER

Simply study the two pictures overleaf. They may at first glance appear the same but look closely and you should start to see the differences. There are ten to find in total, so circle them as you go on the second picture. Finally, fill in the coupon below and pop this page into an envelope and post it today. Don't forget you could win a year's supply of Mills & Boon® books—you don't even need to pay for a stamp!

Mills & Boon Spot the Difference Competition
FREEPOST CN81, Croydon, Surrey, CR9 3WZ
EIRE readers: (please affix stamp) PO Box 4546, Dublin 24.

Please tick the series you would like to receive if you are one of the lucky winners

Presents™ ❑ Enchanted™ ❑ Medical Romance™ ❑
Historical Romance™ ❑ Temptation® ❑

Are you a Reader Service™ subscriber?   Yes ❑   No ❑

Ms/Mrs/Miss/Mr ....Initials ....
(BLOCK CAPITALS PLEASE)

Surname...

Address ....

....

....Postcode...........................

(I am over 18 years of age)   F8C

Closing date for entries is 31st December 1998.
One application per household. Competition open to residents of the UK and Ireland only. You may be mailed with offers from other reputable companies as a result of this application. If you would prefer not to receive such offers, please tick this box. ❑

Mills & Boon is a registered trademark owned by Harlequin Mills & Boon Limited.

The Sunday Times **bestselling author**

PENNY JORDAN

TO LOVE, HONOUR &

BETRAY

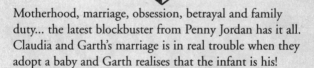

Motherhood, marriage, obsession, betrayal and family
duty... the latest blockbuster from Penny Jordan has it all.
Claudia and Garth's marriage is in real trouble when they
adopt a baby and Garth realises that the infant is his!

*"Women everywhere will find pieces of themselves in
Jordan's characters."*

—Publishers Weekly

MIRA®

1-55166-396-1
AVAILABLE FROM JULY 1998

PENNY JORDAN
COLLECTOR'S EDITION

The *Penny Jordan Collector's Edition* is
a selection of her most popular stories,
published in beautifully designed volumes
for you to collect and cherish.

*Available from Tesco, Asda, WH Smith, John Menzies,
Martins and all good paperback stockists, at £3.10 each -
or the special price of £2.80 if you use the coupon below.
On sale from 1st June 1998.*

Valid only in the UK & Eire against purchases made in retail outlets and not in
conjunction with any Reader Service or other offer.

30ᵖ OFF
COUPON
VALID UNTIL: 31.8.1998
PENNY JORDAN COLLECTOR'S EDITION

To the Customer: This coupon can be used in part payment for a
copy of PENNY JORDAN COLLECTOR'S EDITION. Only one
coupon can be used against each copy purchased. Valid only in the
UK & Eire against purchases made in retail outlets and not in
conjunction with any Reader Service or other offer. Please do not
attempt to redeem this coupon against any other product as refusal
to accept may cause embarrassment and delay at the checkout.

To the Retailer: Harlequin Mills & Boon will redeem this coupon at
face value provided only that it has been taken in part payment for
any book in the PENNY JORDAN COLLECTOR'S EDITION. The
company reserves the right to refuse payment against misredeemed
coupons. Please submit coupons to: Harlequin Mills & Boon Ltd.
NCH Dept 730, Corby, Northants NN17 1NN.

9 904170 250306 >

0472 01316